The Tower

Debra Baker is a Drama graduate from the University of the West of England. She has, in her short time on this earth, always taken an interest in the creation of fictional worlds through different media. *The Tower* is her first novel, and is a meditation on surreality and truth, inspired by a study of Surrealist drama, art and philosophy. It follows one unnamed female character trying to make sense of a nonsensical world.

The Tower

Debra Baker

Arena Books

First published in 2009 by Arena Books

Arena Books
6 Southgate Green
Bury St. Edmunds
IP33 2BL

www.arenabooks.co.uk

Debra Baker
The Tower
1. Reality – Fiction. 2. Fantasy fiction.
I. Title
823.9'2-dc22

ISBN   978-1-906791-28-5

BIC categories:- FA

Printed and bound by Lightning Source UK

Cover design
by Jason Anscomb

Typeset in
Times New Roman

1

The worn wooden desk seemed to sigh as the man shifted his chest onto his arms, making it support even more of the man's body weight. Even gravity was an intolerable force to him, and to everything else that had been tossed into this room and forgotten about; all around the dingy, circular stone walls, not even the cobwebs could support their own existence for the inexplicably heavy air that circulated, and they lay, like most things in the room, limply on the floor. The few items of furniture – two hard backed simple chairs, with threadbare cushions, and that simple, stained desk – sagged under the pressure of their existence, and the pane in the window lattice had also suffered somewhere along the line, with shards and splinters scattered equally on the cold floor inside and whatever was below outside. Very little could be distinguished through the darkened and fractured portal to the outside world; the man doubted very seriously whether there could be anything beyond it, and if there was, that it could be any different from the dreary interior that had come to be his living quarters. Amongst his sleeping-things, consisting of many rags and other odds and ends derived mostly from broken clothes that had been defeated by time, there lay one particular piece of material that he would droop over the hole in the wall at night, to block out an unfaltering and indistinguishable light from outside. For, even though there was little light in this little place, complete darkness was never permitted to consume the space: eternally, it seemed, there would be this dank squalor illuminated into awareness by a light of equal torture to the eyes. Spending its time alongside the man in his solitude were a few items – fragments of a former life – that, now, he refused to take comfort in, and instead shunned to the darkest spot of the whole room.

The man looked down at the page on the desk through wide eyes that had been cut open by pain. He looked down at that white page that stared back at him in remarkable brilliance, with such whiteness that it became a candle that promised light to his shadowy world. He looked down at that page, apprehensive about dimming that light with the ink that sat next to it. He stared for quite some time, taking in the breadth of the task at hand. He dipped the quill slowly into the ink, considering, at the highest level of concentration, a level that had not been required from him in a long time. He paused, and in these tentative moments he dared not breathe. He closed his eyes and brought the implement to hover above

the paper. He opened his eyes in fractions, bit his lip, exhaled and began
to write in a language that he thought he had forgotten.

> MY dearest,
> It has been – longer than I thought I could imagine. Do you still
> remember me? I can understand. I can.
> This time without you cannot break me. I will stay true to you in
> every movement, in every thought in every day.
> I know
> I know you do not remember me. But I will love you, as I always
> have.
> I always
> I am not sure I know. I am not sure I know who you are anymore.
> Did I ever?
> Do I still remember you? Will you understand?
> Could I ever call you by your name?
> I do not know how to sign my name to you, so forgive me. I shall
> just be –
>
> Yours ever true

He had no envelope within the desk in which to send what he had
written (for he was sure that what he had written needed to be sent in
some fashion or another), yet this, truly, was irrelevant, because there was
not even a system in which letters could be sent to the outside world. It
was then, after only a few moments of hesitation due to the shock of
committing liquid thoughts to the solid universe that he drew himself up
onto his feet with great effort. The desk let out a squeak of relief as the
man took back the task of supporting his own weight unaided. A few
shuffled steps and he was at the window, clutching his bright shining
paper like a toddler to a teddy bear, and he began to consider the best
ways of freeing the paper into the outside world. Distantly, his memory
stumbled on an old and worn box from his childhood, inside which a few
distorted images presented themselves of children folding paper to make
them soar through the air. Over space, water even…and he looked down
at his own sheet of paper, and stared, his eyes somewhat glazed in the
consideration of his own flying paper toy. Looking from it to the cracks
in the glass, he shook his head gently to dispel the images from his
internal eyes and decided against defiling the paper's pureness any
further. He moved closer in inspection of the window's state, then gazed
through it to try to make out an impression of the world beyond, only to
be greeted by his own distorted, peering face, and strange shapes and dull
colours that could not be fitted together to create anything of use in his

mind. Defiant to complete his task, he lifted the piece of paper up to a thinner crack in the glass, through which he managed to fit the paper without having to fold or crease it in any way. He looked at it for the last time, with mixed feelings, then let it go, to a fate that he could not anticipate. He could not do anything for quite some time but stand and feel his emotions creep around his skin and delve deeper in, much deeper.

He felt himself, as if in a departure from his human form, begin to crumble, slowly, and piece by agonising piece. Whatever tension in his shoulders and his neck that had not surrendered to the sweet liquidity of hopelessness was gently eased, and left. His head fell like the setting sun to find comfort in his chest. Each vertebrae abandoned its duty to keep the man upright and surrendered to fatigue. He found himself crumpling, as if some omnipotent and invisible force were squashing him down with its little finger, until all the man could see was the familiar sight of the cold cobbled floor in stark, grey detail. Whether it was due to the intense feelings he felt within him, or the effort that hope costs, he remained there, and allowed the harsh cold of the floor creep over him like frost.

Whenever life was kind enough to grant him sleep, the long broken man dreamed of that paper's journey. He saw it falling, gliding peacefully at first, allowing the sun to shine on every letter he had carefully chosen to mark on its surface, and this made him happy; and yet, as was the case when feeling any sort of relief from his otherwise unbearable existence, the reality of his depravity and loneliness grabbed hold of him even in his dreams, and the piece of delicate paper was brutalised by savage winds that twisted and twirled it in ways that were no longer beautiful. It ceased to soar like a triumphant bird, carrying an important message wound around its leg, it was beaten with clubs made of air, whirlwinds that sucked it in and tore it – tore at its very fibres! – so that it could no longer be recognised. It was at this point of change, where one could not salvage any of the past to recreate something meaningful for the present or the future that the winds stopped: and the paper fell out of the sky. It fell, and had not the dignity of landing, but simply plummeted recklessly, and would be doomed to do so eternally. It was these dreams that always left the man with a tear upon his cheek when he awoke, a feat that could not be done anymore by dreams of the past, of all those forgotten things that could be no more. What he really saw was himself, drifting from where he had come from, struggling, with no feasible end in sight.

Unfathomable to him was even a minute detail of what actually happened to that falling, marked dove; and although to him, it kept falling, the truth was much different. It did land, and it was read.

2

It was much calmer today, she thought to herself, looking around her with a familiar smile. She enjoyed these boat trips, and relished the responsibility to set the course of their travel and manoeuvre the vessel to her own preferences. Her gentle, light blue eyes were illuminated like fireworks by the rampant deep red sea that gargled and spat around her. The liquid flames seemed to have pacified within the last few days, and seemed to have been temporarily tamed from their hot ferocity by the young woman's undeniable tranquillity – her mere gaze seemed to soothe any aggressive tendencies that she looked on. Their long boat, with its triangular points at either end that pointed upwards towards the pale blue and white sky, seemed sturdy enough now, and it was quite easy to forget how previously, tidal flames had rushed like rhinos at its sides, and as the boat tipped dangerously towards one side, the young woman's crystal white skin had come into brief contact with the fires below, and had burnt its way through her smooth image of perfection. She diverted her eyes from it as she pushed on gently with the oars, and put the thought out of her mind. She resumed that pleasant smile and swayed her head from side to side in time to the gentle temperament of the fiery sea.

She took a moment, while basking in the aesthetic pleasure that she found in her setting, to glance at her companion, who sat at the opposite end of the boat. Shadow was dressed head to foot in a dark hooded robe, and intended to be to the world little more than a name, a vague image that nothing definite could be attached to. The woman cocked her head to one side to survey her companion for what must be, she surmised, the thousandth time; yet only dull black material met her eyes, just like the thousand times before, and nothing more. She always felt that some sort of message could be read in Shadow's posture, but the heap simply sat still as a rock, and weaved through the sea as a non-functional part of the boat. She had spent a great deal of her time on these journeys wondering about Shadow's state of mind, feelings towards her, and the mystery's life in general: for not once had a word been uttered from underneath those cloaks, and never had there been a situation which ever seemed to be perfect for the silence to be broken. It was after the exhaustion of this mental avenue that led the woman, within a mere month, to begin to invent a character and history for Shadow, and this proved to be a more fruitful and rewarding pursuit and a better way of thinking of Shadow. She entertained herself that once, this enigmatic soul had believed in the innocence and beauty of all things in this world (for she felt, no matter what unfolded in human society, that there must be some sort of good in people and a natural impulse to believe that of others), had been born to traditional and loving parents, who wanted the best for all of their offspring – maybe two brothers, and a sister too – and that in this vein, Shadow had held ambitions and was well on the way to achieving them. A partner, too. Pets even. A house, an establishment, to call home. Whatever the story was that the woman created that day, the climax was always the same: Shadow had had something, something cherished dearly, which was lost or taken away, and it was for this reason these morbid robes had been taken up one day, in exchange for a former life, and not a word had uttered forth from those lips since. And despite being a youthful and hopeful soul, this conclusion always brought a touch of sadness to the woman's mind, which she had to shake off every time, and returned the subject of her thoughts to somewhere near the start of that day's tale, with a renewed effort to tell it differently, any way that did not end up with Shadow sitting silently before her.

Her mind had drifted momentarily to the kinds of things Shadow would say if words were to be formed by a voice that she had never heard, when, for whatever natural impulse within her, she looked skyward. Fluttering up above her was a low flying bird, which she slowed her rowing pace to admire in its full beauty. The thought of such a delightful creature paying the two companions a visit greatly lifted her spirits and was successful in putting out of her mind any unpleasantness that had stained her thoughts. Mesmerising as the bird's twirling and mischievous flight was, she squinted with confusion, as it seemed the bird was in some sort of trouble, and descending in a rather awkward manner. She stopped the boat's momentum altogether in order to further consider the distress above her, and it soon became obvious that her initial impressions were wrong. She waited with patience and wonder as the piece of paper drifted downwards and landed, softly, at Shadow's feet.

Most intrigued by this turn of events, thoughts appeared in the woman's mind like a toy shop full of jack-in-the-boxes that were let loose by an over-excited child. Her excitement rose to find out the nature of what lay before her, and as she stretched out her hand to closer examine the object of her surprise, Shadow moved. This alone was enough to stop the woman from moving any closer, and as she paused, she watched the robed arm of her companion reach out slowly, as if the item was alarming or frightening in some way, and pick up the piece of paper, which then became subsumed within the mass of black that constituted Shadow's attire. It did not seem – although she could not be sure – whether the document had even been glanced at, and because of the large hood and Shadow's natural deflated physicality that included a continual and unfaltering gaze at the floor of the boat, the woman could not read any facial expression, and she doubted whether she would ever see the page again. Immediately, she took up the oars, conscious of the silence and stillness that she had maintained after Shadow had taken the page, which she felt would almost definitely make it apparent that she had been lost in thought, and to cover this, she began to sing quietly. Her thought remained, however, with the unexpected guest to their little trip, and as the woman began to steer the boat around to complete the return journey, she wondered from whence the page had come: her thoughts darted like an unsatisfied bee through a field of inadequate flowers: Had it fallen from the sky itself? Did that ever happen? Had it been arranged by Shadow? Or was it even a delivery for the troubled traveller, arranged by a third party? There could be merit to this idea, she thought, for why else was it that Shadow appeared every week to take this journey with her when it did not seem to her that the journey was ever enjoyable for this reticent stranger, and when she could see nothing in her own manner that would attract such an unprecedented and regular appointment? Her eyes danced over the softened flames, which lay ensconced, lapping tiredly at the sides of their boat; she followed with her eyes the direction of the slight waves to one of the dismal looking stone towers that rose out of the searing sea. Menacing and lonely as it was, the woman couldn't help but admire the defiance of the bold tower, which revolted from the fiery depths below with its own brand of cold solitude. She did not know how many of the towers stood in this vast expanse of interweaving yellows, reds and oranges, and, now that her mind was on the subject, and contemplating the way they sat in and contributed to the environment around her, she wondered what was held within them; she had always thought them to be purely decorative – purposeless entities that served as (if anything at all) demonstrations of mankind's instinct to conquer its surroundings. This was probably the source of their defiant air, but it seemed these towers did not want to be there, and their sagging stones seemed as if they longed to crumble, if only they had not been built with such sturdy materials and science. The boat pushed forward around the tower she had been contemplating from afar, and she considered, as she saw the small and simple dock that was the only means of entering the tower, whether these towers were used as emergency relief for travellers who became caught in treacherous sailing conditions. She knew well the perils of the flames below, and the waves never let sailors forget the potential disaster even in the calmest of times: the occasional licking of the upper edge of the boat reasserted the status of the seas. Even being, as they were, servants to the mood of the temperamental fires, it still seemed a gargantum effort to build such extravagant buildings just for the pluckiest adventurers who knew full well the dangers of their travels before embarking. The two travellers sailed clear of the tower, and now entered the last leg of their journey; yet the woman still stole a few glances back to the tower that they would leave behind to suffer the boiling currents, wondering what secrets might lie therein. They coasted their way back without much trouble from the perilous fires, the dangers of which the woman had almost entirely put out of her mind. Out here, she felt sheltered by a bizarre air of serenity, despite the hazards; after the tension of the silence presiding between the two individuals had subsided, the woman always felt liberated by the sheer expanse of the outside world, and intrigued by all the sights and sounds that passed by.

The boat slid tiredly into the main dock, to once again accompany its brothers and sisters that sat in a proud line. The woman sat still for quite some moments, overheated with rowing and exposure to the raw flames, in order to gain composure. It was the ritual, at this point, for her to leave ahead of her companion, for Shadow would not get up until she had disappeared from sight; coincidently, on arriving for the weekly boat trip, the woman would always arrive with the robed individual readily sat in position on the vessel, so that due to these practices, the woman had never seen the robed mystery anywhere but attached to the boat. She thought that if she were ever to see Shadow without the boat, she would find the instance so alarming that she would lose the power of speech entirely. Now though, as she went to step back onto dry land again, she was struck in the same way she always was: her mind wanted to say something, to communicate anything to this poor, and obviously tormented existence, but her mouth stayed firmly shut. She lingered momentarily, looking as if she could see through the mass of black folds and catch the slightest indication of Shadow's thoughts. Then she turned away. She walked with fatigue in her step, and thought warmly of her home, which filled her with a deep desire to collapse on her bed the moment she had fastened her door shut. A calm smile lit up her face as she passed through the doors that led into the building, and she thought no more of the figure that sat some distance behind her, still and silent in the lifeless boat.

3

That innocent face, with its short dirty gold hair which clung about her ears, and swimming blue eyes that could melt the most stubborn of hearts, now looked upon the front door of a stately gentleman's apartment. Having slept through the latter part of the previous evening and straight through the night – sacrificing the nourishment of her evening meal – she had been awoken with a start this morning by the piercing scream of her alarm clock, that had jumped about the side of her bed, in order to startle the fair woman into action, with eventual success. Despite the early hour at which she was forced to rise, her body felt fully rested, and her mind at ease, due to the over-compensation. After dismissing the initial sleepiness, she fell into the monotony of her routine and rushed from one place to another, preparing herself for the day's work. Her apartment was like all the others in the complex, that were known as units, and was a square room in essence, inside which an inner circular wall sat, leaving the corners of the square to be taken up with smaller spaces: two of which were built-in cupboards (one for food and utensils, one for clothes and other items), one a small space for a toilet and sink and the other a shower compartment. Along one wall, opposite the door, was the kitchen space, which was kept tidy and clear, thanks in part to the abundant storage facility and also due to the minimal cooking items that the woman owned. The walls, however, were the most striking feature upon entering and considering the space; they were painted (as was every unit) with detailed and brightly coloured murals, that were so extraordinary that the woman herself, despite seeing the place everyday, was still struck many a day doing nothing else but admiring the sight of them. Upon taking up residence in a particular unit, the walls transformed their fantastic colours to generate images of the things that made the tenant feel happy, and so it was that all the sources of the woman's happiness were painted upon the walls, fading into each other, creating a vast conglomerative wash of interweaving ideas. Now, however, she dashed around the room, the murals blending into one colour out of the corner of her eyes as she sought for less inspiring sights. Adorning her plain working clothes, she tamed the alarm clock - that was still agitated after the woman's immediate reluctance to heed its call - into its day time hibernation, and locked the colour behind her.

She knocked lightly at first on the gentleman's door, but after waiting patiently for some moments, felt that a louder disturbance might be necessary to entreat the man to notice her presence. On a third attempt, after which the woman would have been out of ideas as to how to draw the man from his present occupation, thankfully the door was opened. After recognising the dainty woman, dressed in her formal black dress with cleaning towels and a bucket of water, he let her pass, and resumed his position in a cosy armchair to engross himself once again in his book. The woman began to busy herself with cleaning the unit in her thorough way; despite the other cleaners' moans about the tasks they had to complete, she enjoyed her job, and could see no reason to complain the way that the others did. She took pleasure in taking the dirty, the broken and the unloved and making them better, leaving each unit sparkling and new again. She relished the reactions that she received – especially, it must be noted, from those elderly residents, one of which she was presently cleaning for – and the thanks that she got for renewing the units in her charge, even on occasion accepting, gratefully, a coin or two tip from those that pitied her relative poverty and also appreciated her service. More than anything, she thought, it was not so much that these people desperately wanted their homes cleaned to a pristine standard, but more that they enjoyed her company, and the infectious smile that she wore upon her face at all times, that brought light into their homes much brighter than any shine they might have upon their porcelain.

Presently, the elderly gentleman shifted in his chair and turned his eyes towards her. She had cleaned for Mr James every week for as long as she had held the position, and although he was often taciturn, preferring mostly to absorb himself in whatever task he chose that day, he occasionally spoke to her as she worked, and always thanked her vehemently when she left. On this occasion, he lifted his eyes above the page and looked over to her while she sorted out the glasses and mugs into their rightful places in the cupboard. Busy with her current objective, she did not see how Mr James stared thoughtfully at the floor, a frown upon his face, considering what seemed from his face a complex and troubling problem. After the woman had finished cleaning and setting right everything in the kitchen, she span around to move onto the shower cabinet, where she was taken somewhat aback by the intensity of the old man's stare. Her movements stirred Mr James from his line of thought and he then directed his thoughtful gaze at the young woman who had begun to scrub the tiles and restore brilliance to them once again. "It ain't right," he murmured, quietly at first, and after getting no response from the cleaner, raised his voice slightly to make it clear that he was not simply mumbling to himself. "What d'you reckon," he put to her, his head to the side, staring into the corner of the ceiling, "about this: that this man, in this here book that I be reading, he turns his back on his lover and goes against all his beliefs 'cause he's tortured by these people. Now how can he let that happen, eh?" The woman sat back on her feet as she considered what the man had said. She did not know what her opinion would be worth to the gentleman, who now held her intently in his gaze, and faltered, "Well, Mr James, I'm sure we would all be driven to things we can't imagine by different circumstances. Torture, I mean – how can we imagine it, you and me here, privileged as we are not to know such troubles?" Mr James patted the book as he considered her words. "Could there be such a situation," he said back at her, "could we ever experience anything that would be that bad that'd make us completely forget who we are though, and deny the existence of our true selves? I mean..." At this point the gentleman leant forward in his chair, his hands gesticulating, trying to grab hold of the answer that the conversation searched for, "I know it's bad an' that. No one wouldn't never say it wasn't, but this guy, in here, he doesn't even think inside himself that he is who he used to be, he's completely changed, he's not even pretending, he means it. Those are some sick bastards, that's sure for definite, if nothing else is," he said, reluctantly settling for an easier and more tangible truth. The woman nodded her head, murmured, "Mmmm," and turned back to the tiles, the distant and contemplative look on her face reassuring the man that she was genuinely interested in the issue that he had raised. At length, Mr James deflated, as if trying to breathe the rest of his strength into coming to a conclusion about the matter, but at the necessity to take in air, he leaned back in his chair, resumed his attentions to the book, and muttered at intervals, "the sick bastards."

The woman steadily moved from room to room completing her tasks, admiring her reflection in every polished surface, and yet, there remained in her eyes the quiet reflection and thought about what the old man had said. It may well have been a simple absent minded attempt to make pleasant conversation, and, as the woman repeated to herself as it lingered on through the day in her thoughts, it had no reason to trouble her or preoccupy her thoughts as it did, but there was something about the nature of self that instigated a lot of activity in her mind. She had never really had to consider ideas like the nature of her own identity and core beliefs before: it was something that was simply not needed for general day-to-day life. All she needed to retain in her mind were the halls that were within her responsibility for that day and which cleaning fluid to use where. When she conversed with the other cleaners, which she did on occasion, during her breaks throughout the day, it was about simple things, such as how Mrs Joyce was getting on, or how the order of new scourers was well overdue, and that their superiors should take heed of the problems that this presented. Never did they offer conversation on lofty issues, and in some ways, although she was a deep thinking woman, she had never really considered, for example, what she saw as her 'true self', and how she lived up to this blueprint. She imagined herself, on many occasions during her working day, how she would fit into Mr James' dilemma, and whether she would give up everything she knew of herself under the right pressurised circumstances. A question that was hard for her to contemplate at first; she saw nothing that stood out about herself from anyone else, and so assuming someone else's identity, say, a fellow cleaner's, would probably not provoke any attention in anyone. And yet she thought, there were things that set her apart from others, her natural good will, optimism, shyness: whereas others could often be quite the opposite, and she thought it would be extremely odd to inhabit such opposing characteristics. But what would she give for who she was? Under pressure of torture, would who she was really be that important to her?

She surmised that the elderly gentleman must be desperately attached to the ideal of people remaining true to their cause, and never betraying this despite life's surprises and sickening turns. Yet she had known, in her young life, those that had changed drastically due to an altered state of affairs, which could turn the devoted into revenge seekers, and the moralistic into the decadent. It was not that she held no faith in human kind, quite the opposite, but she was aware, at least, of its ever pliable nature, and its tendency for surprising and drastic changes. Before she knew it – for engaging thought is often a very effective way of passing time, in a way that one is almost asleep to the physical world – she had finished her last room, and was making her way home. There, she rested, cooked her dinner, and let her mind relax from its general buzzing in the day that had made her quite weary.

As the sun was just setting, she took it upon herself to take a walk – a pastime that she often indulged in, due to having few friends and family members to entertain her or indeed entertain, and also her enjoyment of the crisp evening air. Plunging her room into darkness and closing the door, she walked, her hands in her trouser pockets, along the corridor to the many flights of stairs that led her to the top of the building. Her young, athletic body took the seemingly unending stairs with ease, yet she could not help but notice a twinge of pain in her back from the laborious nature of her work, and so she slowed her pace to compensate. With her hand massaging the small of her back, she emerged into the open air, and she stood still, eyes closed, to let the cool wind blow a smile onto her face.

The building itself was odd in design: it was simply an enlarged circular wall, which held more than twenty units high, and four units wide. It was made from the same sort of enhanced stone that the towers were made of, and its colossal circumference contained both the raging flame sea and the towers that stood within it. It would take many hours to walk from one point of the wall all the way around to meet one's starting point again, and so as the woman sat out at a casual pace, she sought out a point in the distance where she felt it appropriate to stop, rest and then return home. All along the walkway were bright lamps that hung from poles that shone red, and illuminated the path before her; the edges, to prevent people plummeting unintentionally into the steaming flames below, were reinforced with further stonework partitions which came up to just below the woman's shoulders, and allowed her to consider the scenery beyond with ease. She paused many times, on her pleasant perambulation, to look over the wall, and watch in a mesmerised state the pattern of the waves below. The sight was most remarkable: the scene itself was a competition of light and darkness, for while the sky was now as black as the woman's shadow, the moon, full and serene, shone gently on the world below to disturb the darkness. The red lamps mixed with this white light, and created battle lines over every possible object that could be lit. As the woman passed soundlessly through the night, her features were caught in some places by white, and others by red: she appeared as a doll, white as bone, with colour bleeding over her, searching to conquer her as she moved closer to the next lantern, and relinquishing its grasp as she passed it. She watched the fires below wrestle and spit, themselves, of course, bright as day, amongst the darkness that hung over the towers quite naturally. Their conflicts struck like lightening into the air, and onto the walls of the melancholy towers, as flames would unexpectedly leap metres upwards, longing to defy their confined condition, and repeatedly assaulting the stones of the towers as if it were possible for them to climb up and conquer all within their grasp. The stones, having been treated like those of the great wall, by a complex process the woman did not understand, would not take the flames, and never would, and yet still they tried, longing to devour the buildings and declare them defeated.

All this unravelled like an epic tale before the woman, who lost herself in the struggles between the rage of the flames and the serenity of the dark towers. A gentle chilly breeze swept the walkway free of debris, and weaved through her hair, across her whitened skin, swirling as it did around her body, entering into her soul. What liberation could be found in surrendering oneself to the personality of the wind that took her where it willed, and freed her limbs and muscles from their aching prison! She let her arms leave her sides and surrendered them to the pace of the wind that swept with more energy around her, closing her eyes tightly shut and swaying her head from one side to another in complete unbridled freedom. Within her own whirlwind, she fell and rose like a leaf, moved now by a much strengthened force that pushed its rights as puppet master to the limit. She began to forget who she was, and felt only the wind around her - she lost her sense of where her arms and legs were, how she was connected to them, and how she might command them again, for all she desired was to be subsumed within the breath that had lured her as soon as she emerged into the open air. As her eyes twitched open by slight degrees, and her mind began to embrace the complete ecstasy of blankness, delivered from the pain of incessant thought, the wind let its puppet drop, and died down into passivity, a night's gentle exhalation.

She found herself resting, half sat, half led, against the cold wall that offered her no such escape; indeed its stones seemed so cold that the woman felt herself almost to be frozen to it, as if it were an ice cube on the tongue. She had not time to extricate herself, however – the world still appeared to her in a wild blur, and she felt somewhat dazed by the last few minutes – before she heard footsteps approaching her. As her eyes caught up with her ears in recovering their ability, she could see (albeit somewhat lopsidedly, for her head was somewhat at an angle) a figure dressed in black, or rather a kind of red-black, as it appeared in the light, with a formal black cap. As the sound grew louder, the shoes got bigger and bigger, until they completely eclipsed the rest of the person. Her sight was brought sharply into contact with the figure's face – a young, moustachioed man – that eyed her with a puzzled and concerned look. "Are you alright, ma'am?" he asked tentatively, in a deep voice, which fitted perfectly with the rest of his persona, in that he sounded exceptionally formal, and of an upper class background. Her line of sight was jolted drastically from whence it rested, as the man attempted to shift her body into a more appropriate sitting position. Her dumbstruck face met with his puzzled expression, and he repeated his question again. The necessity of the woman to regain her senses at this point overcame her, and she nodded, trying to calm the wild look in her eyes by focussing deliberately on the man's nose, and putting on a slight frown, which she hoped would convey to him her confusion at being in such a strange state along this plain path. She smiled weakly, and this sufficed to convince him, although later she considered how sane she must have looked, frowning and smiling as she did. As he knelt beside her, he pulled out something from his pocket, and announcing, "There is a message for you ma'am, one that requires your most urgent attention, if you would be so kindest." By now, she decided to hazard to her feet, and as the man rose with her, he handed her a letter, promptly took his hat off to her, smiled with a pleasant "Thank you ma'am," and walked off at a stately pace. Bewildered, it took her some time before she could process the events of the last two minutes, and eventually turned back to walk home. As she did so, she looked down at the letter she held in her hand; it was folded into thirds, without an envelope, on a paper of such kind that she had never seen before that felt so strange, and was stuck with a seal. Confusion on her face, and the first few staggered drops of rain in the air, she tucked the letter inside her jacket and resolved to open it when she got home.

Locking the door, throwing her rain soaked jacket on the floor, she sat on the end of her bed and ventured to open the letter, slowly and carefully, as to not damage the delicate paper. She read the following over and over, to be sure she was correct to believe what her eyes told her:

Go down to the dock and take the usual boat – inside there will be a box that you need to take to the first tower. The key to the door is in the box. Lock the door as you go in and lock it on your way out. Take the box to the top and leave it there.

Sorry for the short notice. I need you to do this now. I promise I won't ask you to do this again.

From your companion in the boat

4

Consciousness faded into the man slowly, and as it did, and he became aware once again of himself waking, he bid it to leave him alone to remain in his dreaming, unthinking home, but still it came, and he was forced once again to face his continuing existence, shot into awareness of his entire life by a bullet to the head full of memories. An instant rush of emotion shot to his eyes, and burned down his face – for he had become so cold, lying for an undeterminable amount of time with his naked skin against the unforgiving, frozen stones, that his tears warmed his skin – an effect, he felt, that must have been the result of some far-reaching dream, which had stirred something so central to the source of his despair that as his senses came to him, he could not shift the feeling of utter helplessness in everything, of movement or thought of any kind. He searched desperately to uncover the broken threads of the dream, but it had fallen away, invisible and lost to the dull light of the night that was now poking through the holes in the pathetic cloth over the window. He peeled his wet face away from the cold floor and looked up at the window, out of habit more than for any desire to look at the material flapping in the draft, threatening to fly from its place. The white light shone down, catching his right eye, a black hole that glistened with the tears swimming in and around it. Around him everything appeared to be exactly and agonisingly the same: his desire to check his surroundings fuelled subconsciously by a hope that one day he might look up, and find himself in a warmer, brighter place, where his troubles could be lapped away like waves on a beach, dragged back to the ocean to plague his life no more. How he had tried to imagine, in such lonely moments – which occurred to him now more and more often, until he could distinguish no other existence other than this crippling loneliness – such a place, a white cottage that sat amongst the grasses, a little gate that would tap at its post lightly in the wind, a path winding down towards the sand that would rub up against his skin and cleanse him of his past. A place to sit and watch the waves roll in until the night came. Such fantasies, although granting him escapism, were futile, and as the years wore on, the man became less and less sure of what the world beyond those walls was like, and what could happen there. A spasm of pain tore through his neck and his head fell back down to the freezing stone.

As he lay there, his drunken, twitching eyes forcibly confronted with the grey wall, not a thought passed through his mind: fatigued in every way that one could possibly be, even his mind was too exhausted to plague him anymore with the familiar tortures, and he let himself slide into a strange consciousness. His eyes, though they stayed attached to the dreary stone in the wall, seemed to see differently, as if his focus was retreating, little by little, into the air, like a ghost called to heaven. His eyes, their gaze, left their permanent restriction inside the man's head, and slid effortlessly away from his heavy body. Ascending only slightly every few moments, the man became able to see more and more of the room in all its monochrome monotony, until eventually his own body came into view. His own hideously thin and decaying body lay with its tatters pulled around it to hide the horrors that lay within; his exposed skin greying with the cold of the floor. All things that his detached gaze found moulded into one still organism, one sad place that existed separate from any other world, one black room that took on the rest of the world's despair and misery. Stone after stone lay on top of each other, next to identical neighbours, stuck everlastingly together: their dreary pattern aching in the power with which they had been thrust together and moulded to stay that way eternally. And yet, at the point when the man's vision had ascended to its final height at the centre of the ceiling, as if he were a spider looking down on his own life, where every feature of this room looked as if it would never move or change for the rest of time, the stones of the wall began to tremble as if agitated by an outside force. First one, above the window, slid out of position and fell in slow motion to the ground, and then another, and then another from across the room: all of the grey blocks that had laid submissively to the will of the tower made their final plunge to freedom and destruction. From the ceiling, they fell heavily through the air, pelting all that was below with their weight, the cold wind from the night skies permitted to reach inside to whip up the disintegrating room and add to the slow chaos. The man watched his own body as the world imploded on it, watching with total detachment the frozen missiles crash around him, missing by inches his useless, unmoving body. The near wall began to give in below the room he had resided in for so long, so that the floor that he rested upon began to tilt to such a degree that the body started to slide towards the burning abyss that lay below. The fires that beckoned his descending flesh leapt like morbid dancers into the air, smelling the death on this hopeless character, welcoming every second that brought him closer to be consumed by the hungry, burning mouth with a million fiery tongues. The man's arms were splayed out on the floor, as if they could hold on to the slippery stones that were slipping away, but no effort was exerted towards that end, no life was inside that creature that could save him from being tipped into incineration. His arms, like frail sticks, were wrenched over to the other side of his body as he began to roll off of the very edge, through a rapidly growing hole in the wall. It was now that he would plummet downwards, just like the stones, as grey and cold as them: yet something about the hovering spirit could watch no longer as a bird in the air, and the man's vision snapped instantly back into his own eyes, only to open doubly wide to glimpse for a few seconds the fiery pit that laughed at him, that spat at him, longing to lick his face, and the blackness within it that promised his ultimate, final, doom.

                                                       Um…Excuse
me?

He opened his eyes; or rather, he thought he opened them, but he found, upon doing this supposed action, that he already had his eyes open, and at no point had they been closed. They were dry, hot, and staring at full capacity at the stone in front of him on the floor. He felt entirely wild. He felt not of this world, yet still a voice, like a hook through his head, lurched him back to it.

Hello?

…Sir?
Are you alright?

Minutes swam around him in the air; a storm of silence into which his irregular, scared breath permeated, that kept coming, kept reminding him of that swirling, cackling cauldron of flames that longed to devour him entirely. Sharp inhalations came faster, shorter – the flames screaming in his mind – there he saw himself, falling, falling – to be destroyed without a trace – in – the first burn upon his forehead – those grey stones forcing him down – in – the dreaded dance of fire – the eyes, they stare at me – in – in – my first time – out out out – the burning air – my last time – in – take my lungs – in - never to wake up – take my skin – in – take my body – in – never to die another day – in – never to fall again

                    and all the times
                              I did it
          I did it   I'm so sorry
     there's no
                              the fires
                         I wished
     for it
                                   they gave it
                                             oh

                              forgot
     am I the one
          why did I do this to you
          why do I keep stopping   forget
          why do I keep starting
                              god help us
                    all of us   all of the broken   am I the
broken

let me go

         where to go

    nowhere to go

              why don't you let me go   I

want to be

what could I be

          they gave it

            and   where   could   I

hope go

    hope go

        hope goes away   forget

       I watched

           the fires

oh the fires

    god the fires

         where did the fires come from

    what is fire   what am I   what are you   can

you forgive me

hope goes away in fire

          they gave me

      hope burns away in fire

        am I guilty

I watched myself

     I

        watched

      myself

            BURN

and I…..

love it but I hate it I want it but I can't take it why can't I land why can't I land I always fall nowhere to fall only life and death and nothing in between why can't you help me why can't I burn forget forget forget live cold decaying in my own life you an angel sent for me to take me did my

time come I can't take it now my hope has gone today I lost my hope you
HAVE to take me now my hope is gone I have to go there is no use

angel
take my mind
leave my body here

                                                    am I guilty

OH MY GOD IN HEAVEN THE FIRES ARE COMINGthey're   coming
to

                                                get
                                                me

no going back
no going back
no going back no no
going back now
no going back no going going
I'm going
no going back

        Calm -
no going-
…
…
…
…
…
…
….

                                                It's okay.

Sssssst-

                                                Sssh
                                                now.

                                                It's okay,
                                                there's no
                                                need to
                                                worry.

Don't make yourself
panic,
you'll work yourself up
even more.

You –

You

can   tell   me
what is wrong,
if you want.

Don't feel you have to

do anything.

Okay?

oooo…

o.

okay.

There.

Just breathe –

in
    and

       out.

        In
    and
out.

in..
and…
in!
and!

Out...

ooooooouuuuuuuuuuuuuuuuuuttttt......

in.
and.
out.

The man's intent, unseeing stare retreated back into the realm of reality to find himself looking up at the face of a stranger. A curiosity was born within him like a breeze stirring up dead leaves, and he looked up at her through bulging, bright eyes, that drunk in her smooth, delicate skin; her sweet, forgiving blue eyes that requited his gaze; her short, blonde strands of hair, the majority of which were pulled behind her head into a cute bob. He lay, as he realised after spending some minutes staring into that white, innocent face that seemed to attract his gaze like a magnet, in the arms of this woman, her hands supporting his head, delivering it from its prolonged exposure to the cruel stones that seemed always to be cemented to one part of his body or another. Slowly, he began to reclaim conscious control of the rest of his body: he took a quick look out of the corner of his eye to see the mingling of his own, partially exposed bony frame with that of the young woman's, her white flowing cotton clothes draping areas of his skin. His head snapped back to meet her eyes again, his eyes now unsure, his expression darkening, until, in one definite and unplanned movement, he launched himself away from her, scuttling with fearful urgency into the darkest part of the room. Crawling into himself, looking back through scared eyes like a frightened mouse, the man began to tremble, and watched the woman's every move until she left.

The woman stood, disturbed by her encounter thus far already, distressed by this odd creature's extreme mood and the radical changes in his behaviour. Her eyes fought to find his truth through the darkness that he had attempted to pull around him like a safety blanket; she looked down on a slug of a man, one that was not unattractive by nature, but one – she could tell - who had morphed through time to become the tormented, broken frame she saw before her. She could barely look at man's body, and felt a deep intrusion at noting the way his bones seemed almost to penetrate through the weathered, dirty skin, and hoped that the remnants of his clothing – which in some lights seemed to resemble grey pinstripe trousers, a dull shirt and a tweed jacket – would somehow sew themselves back together to hide his shame and scars of obvious brutality. She looked away briefly – and she would be forgiven for doing so, for only one like her, caring by nature, would have the confidence to look at the man at all and not be repulsed immediately by his squalor – to collect herself, for she did not want her emotions to spill out onto her face where it could so easily make the man's condition worse. She considered his face in a renewed attempt to work him out: her eyes fluttering over an expression that had been fixed downcast and detached, and was only lightened now by the fear that gripped not just his face, but that excited his whole body, and made his heart shake and rattle his bones as if he were a small mammal waiting to be killed. Her calm countenance was disappearing fast as she looked on, as the two strangers stayed locked in their unexpected intimacy: the woman searching now with intensity to find any trace of hope in the trembling man, but every part of him visibly ached, sores and dried blood mixed in with the grime and dirt as if he was sinking into the floor, and becoming less human. She swallowed, and looked back at his eyes. She felt herself freeze over. Those eyes, that looked up with such intensity, held her physically to the spot, and she became completely unable to break the bond they shared – those deep, deep brown eyes that beseeched her yet feared her, that looked up like potholes under which tunnels drove down into the heart of this alien being, into the secrets, the memories, the self that lay protected by all of his barriers and delusions, his words and his silences. 'Who are you?' She wanted to say to him, as if her eyes could communicate in a way that he would understand was not threatening, and would allow her to comfort him so that he could stop living in this torturous state. She wanted desperately to hold him as she had only moments ago, and though she had been encouraged by the calmness that she had been able to impress on him, it was not enough. What was he doing here, and how long had he lived like this? But still those holes in his eyes looked up at her, the void which she could not fill, those huge eyes she could not close and pacify into dreaming a peaceful sleep. And yet still she remained, doing nothing, thinking little, but for those eyes, those eyes that were caught so brilliantly yet unintentionally by the white moon's shining fingers that stretched all this way to touch him, as she longed to do herself. Her shyness, her sense of her own inability to any good in the current situation prevented her from doing so, yet also prevented her from leaving: feeling herself to be an inferior nurse, she could not truly bring peace to such a disturbed mind and yet, she could not take herself away, feeling that to leave him alone, to plunge him once again into dark solitude would also disturb him further. Still those staring eyes, they penetrated into her mind, they never faltered…

She was not aware of how she came to leave, or how long she had spent in that room at the top of the tower. As each foot slowly found each new step down the winding staircase that had delivered her to such strange circumstances, she looked back often – the closed door and the unopened package that she had been instructed to leave stayed frozen in each of their places, never moving, never giving a hint of the timid body caged beyond them. Out she emerged, finally, onto the dock, and her patient boat that bobbed lifelessly on the tame flames. Boarding the vessel and turning home - a barely conscious automatic sequence - her thoughts remained in the tower: as she made the slow journey back, the breeze playing a slow, sad tune around her, the moonlight shone down on a woman clearly disturbed by her chance encounter, who could make no sense from the last hour or more of her life. Her playful smile wiped from her lips, she stared straight ahead, the fires beneath her like purring hellish kittens. Yet she noticed nothing around her. It was only once she was on stable land again she glanced up at the black sky, as if the queen moon had been a third party to her encounter and could give her the meaning she searched for. Yet it was still. Everything was still around her, and cool. As she brought her head down, a blemish on her arm caught her eye: a dirty grey mark on her cold, white skin.

5

"It's just so hard to describe to you," Smoke said, as he looked up at a very specific point in the ceiling, shaking his head lightly at being unable to find the words he wanted, a skill that was usually his forte. He brought his hands together and lifted them to his lips, and then opened them, as if to expel the truth of his thoughts through this action. He laughed lightly, and looked back at the blonde haired woman that sat opposite him across the table. "Sometimes, darling, things just turn out right; you'll find plenty of times where life doesn't work that way, but other times, and these are the ones we have to remember, they.." he smiled and looked deep into her eyes, "they just turn out right." His smile broadened and he lifted his glass to his lips. After replacing the glass, Smoke waved his hand, as if to dismiss that subject from their table, and resumed his deep, considered look at her, which he often adopted in his retreats from being the dominant speaker, in order to fully analyse his sister's expression and language. "But come," he said, propping his chin on his hands, "what about you my dear? If I were a little braver I'd suggest you were still troubled by what you told me a few days ago."

She visibly shifted in her seat, and let out a sigh, and in so doing gave her brother a little more information than she wanted to give him:

although she did not actively hide anything from him - she knew she could not anyway, due to the incredibly accurate and slightly creepy way that he could read her - she still didn't like the idea of baring her soul every time she talked to him. It was the desire to let him know about her life in her own way, and in her own time, which made her wish she was a little more restrained and aware of what certain elements of her behaviour told him. Knowing she did not need to say anything now in order to confirm Smoke's perceptions, she remonstrated herself and resolved to try to reassure him of her position on what she had told him about her meeting with the brown eyed stranger last week. She leant back in her chair and played with the coaster sitting underneath her drink while she spoke, hoping that if he was unable to see straight into her eyes, then maybe he would believe every word: or at least most.

"I do think of it yes, you know Smokey, of course I do..." she started, trying to keep her tone upbeat. "What I think of most often is that while I'm going around, doing my cleaning and things, he's in that tower. I mean isn't it just human nature to be worried?" She looked up, and waited for his nod – he was still looking straight at her, and she could feel the piercing stare on her as she resumed her train of thought, and played with the excess water on the table. "I mean it's nothing out of the ordinary. You...can't help but think why he's there, can you? I didn't even know they kept people in the towers..."

"What did you think they were for?" he said, kindly, and tilting his head to the side, as if intrigued by her naivety.

"Oh I don't know Smokey...is it ever talked about? Do people talk about it?"

"Every now and then I suppose dear...but not many people get sent up there, so we can only assume that is the reason that you didn't know about what goes on up there." He paused and smiled mischievously, "After all the times you must have sailed past and through those stone pillars that stand so proud!"

Her body slumped somewhat and she looked down at her lap. She made another effort at trying to engage him on the subject. "What do you think he could have done?"

His eyes lit up with this prod in the direction of analysis, as he relished the opportunity to push her. "Does it matter to you?"

She thought. "Well...yes, obviously...I don't know if I'd feel less sorry for him though...you should have seen him, Smokey, he didn't even look human anymore, he's completely...he's lost himself..."

Her eyes opened wide, and for some time, she did not blink. Smoke kept on talking, about morality and punishment, but his sister heard none of it: her thoughts went straight back to Mr James and his dilemma, about torture, and what had happened to that poor man at the top of the tower for him to completely lose any sense of himself, and live out an existence entirely different to one he had lived before. At the nearest opportunity, the woman excused herself to the bathroom, lest Smoke pick up on the alarming thought that had just crossed her mind. All sorts of thoughts jumped around, impatiently wanting her attention and time; but as she tried to sedate them so that she could consider them later, one thought remained prominent in her mind – how long had he held on to his identity before existing as he did now, and was there anyway he could get it back?

She returned, in time, back into the bar, which was one of her brother's favourite places: deep purple lighting was fixed to the ceiling in square fixtures, and gave the entire room a unique atmosphere, and the people that the light fell upon were generally disposed to enjoying a quiet drink rather than excessive indulgence. The establishment was a few floors below her unit, and was one of hundreds of bars, clubs, restaurants, shops and general places for entertainment that were scattered around the giant building, which sometimes sat side by side, and in other places camouflaged in amongst residential units. Most of these places were the same size as normal units, although there were certain exceptions for the more lively clubs and pubs. As the woman walked back to her and her brother's table, remembering to resume her familiar smile, she saw that he had put his jacket on and looked very much inclined to leave.

"What's wrong?" she said, gathering up her jacket and bag and following her brother towards the exit.

"Come, dear, usually it's you having to convince me to go out dancing! I've not even had that many drinks, and already I'm the one dragging you out to enjoy yourself!" he laughed, poking her arm in jest.

"Well there's a surprise - I thought you were going to say you'd had enough," she replied, slightly amused at her brother's gesture to distract her from her previously discussed worries. There certainly was something that tickled her about her brother's conduct in the clubs that they went to; she was used, all her life, to the serious side of Smoke, one who loved to think his problems through (as well as other people's, evidently) and find new ways to apply his mental faculties. Yet, once he had passed the age of seventeen, this was no longer always the case, and, as she grew up and their relationship changed to one where they could both be adults and no longer young sister and older brother, she noticed it more and more. She could not tell for certain what his thoughts were about women – it was certain that he had never treated *her* badly, or condescended her in any way just because she was female, but she felt that in all actuality, she was an exception rather than the rule. She had definitely observed that some strange habits and traits only emerged when he went places where he felt he was a hunter on the prowl; and the club they were on their way to was one of the best places to observe such oddities in Smoke. As the evening drew on, both brother and sister surrendered themselves to the pulsating music and the alcohol throbbing through their veins, throwing their hands in the air and performing clumsily a wide range of moves that would make them blush if ever they were to watch themselves doing so. Fatigue began to creep into the woman's body, and after a few hours, left Smoke alone to pursue a tall brunette named Caroline.

The beat was still knocking against the walls of her mind as she managed to haul her heavy body into her unit. Kicking off her shoes and releasing her keys onto her beside table, she allowed herself to sink into her bed like a pebble dropped into a pond, and to the dreams that spread themselves around her consciousness. The stillness, despite the movement of the music in her head, calmed her, and allowed her mind to float in the air as her body, warm and heavy, remained amongst the bedclothes. After flowing minutes of relaxed slumber, lying there as a breathing bed cover, she felt compelled to rise, and look in the mirror – she knew not why, but felt as if it called her, and so she walked over to meet it on the wall. Her reflection bewildered her senses – she moved her head to the left, then to the right, trying to understand the process by which the girl in the mirror copied all her movements perfectly. She felt that face to be entirely unfamiliar to her, and although she wanted to talk to her, she could not find words to speak, nor even sentiments to express other than the need to express something. The woman drew closer to the mirror, and looked unblinkingly at the eyes that stared back at her intently - those black tunnels seemed so familiar, yet they offered nothing to her, and she could not see into them, for there was only blackness. Those quiet dark circles, as she looked at them, began to grow, slowly at first, and then with alarming speed – the blackness began to take over her, and she watched as her entire eyes become coal beads in her head - she could no longer see anything, yet she knew the blackness was still expanding, and advancing over her skin, claiming her limbs and her entire body, until all that would be left was one black marble, inside which she would be crushed and contorted beyond comprehension.

She woke with a start, her desperate breath filling the air, her skin trembling with sweat. Relief faded into her system slowly, as the disturbing impact of the dream did not shift from her mind – she could think of nothing but the image that was real, and frightening, but also unexplainable and unprecedented. She lay awake for an hour longer – by then the morning was well under way and sunrise was but a little time away – to try to recapture some peace that would allow her to slide into a pure sleep, and eventually fell away into blank dreams that did not trouble her.

Yawning through her day at work, she scrubbed clean the surfaces in her charge with extra care for dirt, especially anything particularly dark or black that reminded her of her nightmare, the sight of which had become unsightly and repulsive to her. She probably (on reflection) spent a little too much time maintaining this standard, for many of the elderly residents whom she cleaned for that day remarked on her changed, slower and more considered style that she had adopted, and after a polite explanation about her preceding night, many comments were uttered upon the folly of youngsters and their unexplainable desire for the drink and the small hours. Halfway through her day, she realised that yet again it was the day for her evening boat trip with Shadow, which let her relax a little, and consequently she fell back into her old routine and habits, her serene smile fading onto her face yet again. In amongst the snippets of conversation with residents, her thoughts turned to her previous meeting that mysterious stranger; and of course, the letter that had fallen from the sky and had found its home within the many folds of that black robe. There was no doubt now that that descending page had come from within that tower, and the brown eyed wreck of a man that lived within it, yet her curious mind could not conceive of any likely connection between the two, and she knew, from her experiences from so many weeks sitting opposite Shadow, that she was not about to find out anytime soon. And so her mind kept pushing for answers, and could not be content in simply accepting the circumstances as they were.

For some reason she had expected, despite her resignation to complete ignorance, that something could happen on the boat, that, in accordance with the events that had taken place, including her unexplained summoning at the dead of night, further oddities might come about, and eventually, she might be able to gleam some way of interpreting the world as it spun around her, confusing her perceptions of life and making her feel very different to how she once felt. Yet as she sat there in that well worn boat that became her seat for adventurous wonderings, her thoughts began to run fast and thick, while the world around her barely moved at all: the controlled pace of the boat was not enough, she desperately wanted to work her arms to full capacity to charge their vessel at top speed towards that tower standing tall, to tear through that rising staircase, to help that poor soul locked away from the world, to discover the truth, to see Shadow without that concealing black cloak that locked away anything that could possibly give her the slightest clue as to why she had first been requested to take this strange trip every week, and why this unfathomable desire to journey like this burned with so much passion within those dark clothes to warrant the figure appearing like black magic on that one evening a week. It may not be passion, she thought, that Shadow felt, for it seemed strange that anything of the sort could be felt within that ghostly presence, and that even the robe was filled with anything but air. At first, it had been a greatly appreciated break from monotony and normality; a piece of unheaded paper with a simple request written upon it, in letters that seemed to almost float into the air, away from their occupation on the page – it spelt intrigue, it meant excitement, it was in every form *mystery*, which enticed her curious mind and her daringly inquisitive thoughts, but the affair had continued with nothing added to this initial opening, this offer of an enigma which she longed to break: it remained, unbroken and without a hope of every being understood by her frustrated mind. That was it: it was frustration, pure and simple, she just did not understand, and she felt her brother's presence in her mind when she thought of her desire to know and analyse. She looked around her, yet was too lost in her burying thoughts to notice that the flames rising higher and higher around her, hissing with increasing anger like furious cats, and then screeching louder as the screams of dead sailors seemed to erupt into life with frenzied desperation. She wanted to let out it all out, let out what was fast becoming rage – she felt the flames inside her – to let her vocal chords reach the tops of the towers that looked down on her insignificance and ignorance, which seemed to be mocked by everyone she knew and everything around her. They all knew more; they were more than her – a game that was played around her without her consent. Heat gripped hold of every pore of her skin, moving outwards from the burning felt within her, and she snapped out of her thoughts to watch herself turn red – all her white, delicate skin, roasted by the uncharacteristic emotion she felt within her, a lily engulfed by the flame. The scream was rising in her throat, her fingers were curling into her palms, her eyes were opened with the desire to transfer her torment into the world around her and select a victim – and she had been blinded up until this moment, she realised now, to the world around her, because she noticed with increasing alarm and panic that the sea of ever burning fire was no longer licking playfully at the sides of her boat, but was rising as a frantic, murderous wall of boiling lava that threatened to block out her sight and experience of the world as she knew it. Lurching immediately for the paddles, she did exactly what she had wanted to do, to proceed with extreme speed to the exact place she had wanted to be, yet all of her musings were forgotten in an instant as the flames projected scenes of her last moments of life, the sadistic satisfaction of the consumption of the innocent and young, the devouring of the untainted angel white skin. The woman cried urgently and wildly into the many faces of the fires that shrieked like ravens and longed to burn to ash the young body that defied them – she cried out, with the frenzied effort of forcing the vessel forwards as the spray of the fires began to rain down on her, and tossed her head as flecks of heat spat with contempt from the looming death bringers. The kill was in the air.

6

The bricks of the tower stood, as they always had done, cold and always reaching upwards into a sky that never seemed to offer anything but rain that slipped sadly down each individual stone, licking down years of obligatory adherence to the proud whole. Even at this very moment, drops hurtled down to grace those grey stones again, the run off helping to pacify the violent battle of flames below. The tower, if it had eyes, would look down to see the same scene of red and grey that always lived side by side, never changing, only fluctuating with the rise and fall of the temperamental fires. And though those stones may not have seen – although they certainly felt the heat of the flames' tantrums and explosions on their cold, still bodies – this vastness was contemplated by other eyes, now calmed to their usual watery blue. She gazed out, bewildered, as if all the breath had been evacuated from her body, leaving her completely empty. Few clues could tell her what events had preceded that moment in time, and what had actually happened to her. Her eyes following the now gentle twirls and graceful leaps of the fire, she searched for answers, embarrassed and ashamed of the overwhelming emotion that she knew in her heart had taken over all of her mental faculties. Had she lost control of the boat, just for thinking? What could have happened if she had never realised? She shook her head and swallowed the rising stress in her throat. Her hands went to her stomach. She felt sick.

Every now and then, she would spy uneaten scraps of her beloved boat make a defiant spring upwards, as if they had the power to completely extricate themselves from the bloody battlefield, only to be pounced on and dragged ferociously beneath the current, never to be spotted again. Night had well and truly fallen, and there was no denying that they would have to at least spend the night in this tower, if not longer – she knew, or she had deduced, by the fact of there being many other boats in the main dock that others did sail these turbulent burning seas, but she knew not how often this was done, who would take such journeys, and most importantly, why. The night breeze whistled melancholic tunes through the air, whispering and breathing softly over her. Her eyes turned upwards to the moon hanging delicately in the sky. It seemed even the flames had eaten a piece of her too, for only a white slipper sat on that starry carpet. Her hand slipped down the smooth door to the tower, and she turned inwards to the candlelit alcove that housed the base of the staircase. It was entirely bare but for the two recesses in the wall in which sat the candles she had hesitantly lit with the very entity that had only just threatened their lives. The candles pacified the little baby flames, and she was not fazed by them despite the ordeal. The first step accepted her light frame, and she sat in waiting for Shadow. Throughout the chaos of escaping the sinking boat, she had not really seen the black robes move at all, and could not remember how Shadow had been disengaged from the defeated vessel. The mysterious stranger had ascended the steps of the tower, and she could only assume a meeting was presently taking place in the room above. She had waited for an expansive amount of time, and it was a wonder to her that the sun had not risen and fallen several times in the sheer length of waiting she suffered alone since those quiet footsteps had disappeared to eye and ear. On an aside, it proved to her nonetheless that there was a living being underneath the shroud of mystery. However, to any other wonderings, her mind was tired, like her aching body that was now still, having flailed so manically. She could not bring herself to contemplate what could be happening or what could be being said so high above her; it was just so beyond her grasp, so outside her knowledge that she had no information on which to base any theories or fantasies. It was unknown, unknowable, and she, for the first time in her life, accepted that it was something she could not, and would not know.

Eventually, she began to hear descending footsteps. She stood immediately to let Shadow through once the shrouded presence had arrived, at a painstakingly slowly pace, at the base again. A breeze like death shivered over her cold body as the stranger passed by her. The hood of the cloak covered so much of the head beneath that the woman wondered whether Shadow's eyes could actually see out at the world that was passed through. The tails of the fabric fell so far down they dragged along the floor, leaving absolutely nothing of the real Shadow to breathe in the real world apart from through the blackness. A dark bubble that let nothing in or out. The robes passed by her, and trudged slowly to an area that would have been called a corner if the plan of the building was not circular and prohibited such areas being called such – it was next to the staircase, and in that sense, was the most enclosed portion of the area available. It was there that the robes buckled to allow Shadow to sit against the cobbles. They did not move from that spot, and the only movement that happened for the rest of the night was, presumably, in response to the woman's held gaze at the newly nestled blackness: an arm rose from within, and a gloved black hand emerged: the fingers curled into the palm, the forefinger extended and pointed at her to sit or lie upon the floor. Or at least, this was how she interpreted it, and was what she did, without hesitation. Silence stuck in the air and both breathing bodies were still, as if they could become stone statues if only they remained that way for a few more hours.

She found it impossible to discern whether Shadow was sleeping – and feeling the desire rise within her again to meet the man that haunted the room above, hatched a plan to ascend the stairs at the point where the silence seemed the deepest. Hours passed before she could consider a suitable time to stir: she knew not what would happen if Shadow caught her, and nervousness buzzed within her stomach and throat at the idea. But, she reflected, she could not rest now or ever if she could not see that poor man again, and comfort him in whatever small way she could, even if it was unwanted or in vain – to leave behind a fallen soldier to the gunshots, a wounded bird to the cruel loneliness and separation from the world that he lived every day was not a course of action that she could accept or live with. Yes: all that could be done must be, regardless of the life he had lived to arrive at the top of that cold tower, the way he experienced his days now was not fit for anyone. Holding her breath and gathering up her skirts, she lifted herself in the quietest degrees she could manage; on hearing and seeing no objection to her movement, she made quietly for the steps. Her sequined slippers let out little complaint at being set in motion, and veiled the woman in a silence that allowed her to climb higher and higher upwards. It seemed to take so much longer than the last time she had done so, for now the night was deeper than before, as winter loomed, and it did its best to trick her and pull the stone steps from underneath her cautious feet. As she reached the top, she felt nervousness emerge again, and the thought suddenly occurred to her that her presence in the man's chamber might startle him into making enough noise to wake Shadow below. She stood before the door. Let the breathing subside. And pushed the door open.

She should have realised, before entering, that the man who locked her in that meaningful gaze would not be in any better condition than she last saw him; that in all actuality, he was likely to be a lot worse, look even more moth eaten, more beaten in mind and body, and be even further away from the reality that was carrying on at entirely different speed around him. She considered none of this, but even if she had, she could not have expected what she immediately saw before her, an image slowly revealed to her left to right: the body of the man lay in the middle of the room, unmoving, his bones sticking even fiercer through his skin as if to skewer him from the inside, his arm flailed out to the side of him, his hand facing upwards, cupping a pool of blood. The colour from her face was instantly snatched away as she stared through the cold, dark air: she rushed to shut the door and fell about her knees to check if hope still beat in his veins – how she dreaded as she felt about for a pulse that she had been too late, and her hours of waiting had cost this prisoner his life! Tension held back the tears gathering in her eyes from bearing the drop down her face to be frozen upon the floor: at last, her hands found him, and her fingers pressed themselves up against his vein: she almost fell apart entirely to feel a faint tremble below the skin. Yet he did not seem to be conscious, and she knew not what to do with him – she looked up and down at his cadaverous form in panic and desperation, wishing she was more equipped to save him. She resolved to shake him gently, to see if he had done nothing more than fallen into a faint sleep, but this did little more than rattle him as a forgotten, discarded toy. Focussing instead on the blood that was still shooting steadily into his hand, she quickly turned to tear off a portion of his fraying trousers so that she might bind the source of his wound. As she did so, she let the blood trickle from his hand onto the floor; it ran away over the stones and made its home within the cracks. She sat back on her heels and looked mournfully down at the helpless soul, her hands flying to her face in the shock that was beginning to make her body numb. Stillness and silence added to the stagnant air that had filled the man's lungs for so long and was now finding its way around the woman's. After some time in a state of thoughtlessness, the woman reached for the rags that lay against one of the stone walls and draped them over the starved body. She could think of no more that she could do for him, and so sat as she was, next to him, gently stroking his arm, trying to bring warmth to his shivering skin.

As the night wore on she sat there, an invisible nurse to his condition: she wished to be more, to have some food about her person that she could offer, or bandages that could go some way to at least covering his open wounds, but she could not give any of these things. Sleep did not tempt her, or lure her down the dark steps to resume her place opposite the sleeping Shadow – she wanted to give the little time she could offer to him, for it was the only thing that she had that she could part with. Even as she sat there, a short time incomparable to the seemingly never-ending stretch that his body had been bruised lying on those unforgiving stones, she felt her body droop under the room's atmosphere – she could not understand how such a deep sadness weaved its way into her, but it seemed to weigh upon every part of her body and not just depress her mind: the hand with which she hoped to soothe life into the man became so heavy it was barely capable of movement, and she was forced to rest it still on his weary arm. Her posture had been crushed, as if both ends of her spine were being forced to meet each other, and her head felt compelled to fall forward and hang with the weight of the air above it pressing down. She felt herself – though she could not recollect the instance later – give way to the pressure, and lie down, her eyelids slammed shut to prevent her being aware of the force that caused her to feel so suddenly sleepy. There was nothing to explain it but the oppressive darkness that surrounded the two figures that lay beside each other so closely.

Uughhhhhhh…

What are…

You

doing…

here

It's the white lady
She's come to save me

How are you?

I hurt.
oh god he's going to come and get me again get me he said he would he's going to take my soul and
and
and

I will die

Wait.

I'm going to die die die die I'm he's but I'm

It's okay, just take it
one
thing

          at
            a
          time
       I hurt.

           Where?
           I'll make it better.

No,
No,

No,

       I hurt.
       I hurt.
     it never stops
   there's so much
        so much
   time   there's so much time in the world
this is all
     time that
       I hurt.
time keeps going it would keep ticking but there are no clocks no ticking
but I still know it I know even in the always quiet it's going no one can
fool me time still passes I know
       I know
       I know
       I will die here
oh god
oh god   I'm going
oh god   to die
   I thought you
   were here to save me
           just another dream
    time keeps passing

   dreams keep passing

      away from me

          what do you mean?
I mean I mean I mean they are keeping me here
      who?
    time
    the world

        time
I…

I can't remember.
I wish
       I could
            remember

               everything

but I can't

why am I? wh-
why…
what am I talking
I am talking again

        there's no one here
      why the always talking

           NO ONE'S HERE
          IT'S ALL A DREAM
      it's all a…
            I'm real.
            are you?
                I'm here.
            are you?
                believe me.

             I want
                     to help

             will you let me?

a sweet dream
it's cold here
no place for dreams

         I'M NOT ALLOWED TO HAVE DREAMS
cold
cold
cold

do you have anything else for a blanket?
she speaks still

I am here.
it's okay…

don't be scared, I just want to
help

you

me?
Yes.

really?
Yes.

fickle dream
fade away
I can't believe in you

anymore

Having gained temporary awareness of the world around him, the man softly slid back into sleep, or at least into an inactive state where the woman's gentle words and physical reassurances provoked no reaction or receipt of their existence. She laid there, his words having touched something so deep within her that she could not free the expression of concern and profound sadness from her face, her tender fingers trying once again to massage life into his skin, looking into and beyond his soulless face and wishing despite herself to shine some hope into its features. Yet her entreatments seemed in vain, and her hands fell upon the man as if he were a small splat of grey dough bent cruelly over a broken frame. She could not leave. She could not stop the feelings swirling within her, and as she remained there, they became even harder to ignore: her face shaped his pain, her mouth opened as if to further implore the vacant man to animation, yet no words could be born into the air for the totality in which she experienced her emotions. Her eyes looked down in complete pity, those innocent eyes which had never looked on such suffering before, and could not accept such souls could be committed to such hopeless lives, and still her hand tried to soothe his arm, and still she stayed there, refusing to move, and still she looked at him in complete and paralysing pain. Tears struck the stoned floor like a low, mournful xylophone, and she sat like a deluded mourner by his side, wishing for his life to return to him, for what must have been hours until the sun began to rise. The lone shadow lingered as a ghost by the body of a man who was dead in so many ways. The first ray that peeked nervously through the split glass in the window found only one soul in that room, and looked on him with familiar and stark defiance.

7

The heap of darkness in the makeshift corner below did not appear to have moved an inch since the woman had abandoned the better part of her senses and left Shadow. Here sat silently a being so mysterious - she naturally felt intimidated by the dark presence, and she could not immediately tell whether her disobedience had been noticed at all. She suspected, after passing the initial nervous period of waiting to see what happened that yet again, it was another one of those things that she would never know or understand, and naturally felt empowered by Shadow's lack of action towards anything that she did or didn't do, and felt even embarrassed that she had ever thought she would suffer any retribution for her actions. She thought, as she coyly considered Shadow's appearance that, being so devoid of any characteristics or personality, choosing not to speak and rarely even moving, that Shadow was whatever one projected onto the plain, black robes – a complete blank into which only one's own preconceptions of character were reflected back into one's eyes. Shadow was whatever one wanted Shadow to be – a being that was shaped to the viewer's mind, as dark and definable as one's own shadow. All this being true enough to the woman, she considered with deepening ferocity – an intense curiosity that surpassed the passive speculation that she had indulged in previously – who on earth the person beneath the mirror was: there had to be something or someone there, and what was there that needed to be concealed in such a dark secret? The woman tossed her head impatiently, trying to keep the frustration from taking over her again, and tried to pacify herself by turning her attention again to the situation that both her and her sailing companion were in.

As the morning dawned on the little world that lay in all its morbid beauty, little changed within that tower – the woman sat, supported by the stone walls, awaiting the next movement in the strange story that was unfolding around her; Shadow existed, rather than sat, up against those same walls and despite the stillness, seemed as if trying to resist the embrace of the incoming sun rays; the prisoner upstairs, the woman was sure, was still lying, dipping in and out of a strange kind of existence between reality and dreaming that seemed to be all of his own, a place where no other living thing could exist, or ever would exist again. The day played out as normal for so many people, scurrying about their routines within the outer great wall while those unlikely companions sat, absolved from the monotony of that which kept each day following the one before it in one continuous existence that came to be known as life: they sat marooned as the third eye that watched on, removed from their unconscious selves that repeated the same tasks at the same times every day without fail or relief.

The heat of the morning peaked – sitting as stone statues, embellishments to the still tower that locked them away from the outside world, the woman was able to distinguish the smallest changes to the air, the stone, the silence, the temperature as if it had become an extended part of her body, or her consciousness – and still nothing flowed in transparent waves over the tableau. On a few occasions, the woman managed to snatch a few moments of passing sleep, her growing fatigue overpowering whatever tension still remained in her muscles to resist an imaginary burst of energy or action that she still half expected of Shadow. As the afternoon wore on like the morning had done, with no party ever moving or making a sound even to cough or to clear their throat, the woman achieved a bizarre sort of tranquillity, and allowed herself to trickle through her thoughts untroubled like a stream passing over and between familiar rocks and stones. And then, far away, the world changed slightly – a presence somehow seemed to have broken away from the great standing wall, and was disturbing the air, and set the sea of waves hissing and cackling afresh as they carried upon themselves a new body that blocked out their view of the clear blue sky that was so often the subject of their rage. A boat was undeniably sailing in their direction: the woman hesitantly stood from her unforgiving seat and peeked around the outside door to behold in her gaze a vessel of hope, a deliverance from enforced captivity. A bright young girl rowed alone, her eyes barely moving from an apparently fascinating spot on the bottom of the boat a few inches in front of her feet; her black hair whipped about her face in the slight breeze that had struck up within the last few minutes; her simple clothes, a white blouse underneath which a strapped dress was worn, fluttered in the wind like her hair, independently of her. Her physical being, in fact, moved independently: there seemed to be in her two entirely disconnected halves of one existence. She seemed, the woman thought, to be coming closer to the tower as if her journey were set to music – the striking sight of her set off a searching piano melody in the woman's mind, over which the wind sighed, whispering unintelligible words devoted to that detached girl rowing, who seemed as if she would keep rowing until she fell off the end of the world in a fiery waterfall, into an eternal blackness.

Evidently she must have had some sense of being watched, and allowed herself to be watched nonetheless; for she looked up directly into the woman's eyes, like snow white peeking out from underneath a riding cape. Though their eyes met each other only briefly before the girl's fluttered back down to their former coyness, her deep brown eyes struck the woman as quite remarkable, full and beautiful.

Unable as she was to coax those eyes out again, the woman made an effort to stand near the small dock where the rower might come to steady her vessel – she could tell, by the girl's course, that she fully intended to do such, and it did not seem too much of a presumption to prepare for such course of events to follow. The woman stood, a little unsure of the situation, waiting for the girl to look up again so that she could offer a smile or a small wave – and when this did not happen, and such social practices could not be performed, a sense of confusion came over her, and made her stand uncomfortably. And it was in such manner she lingered, until the anticipated movements came to pass, and the girl sat, a few inches from her.

For some moments she was quite dumbstruck: no phrase, or even word, seemed to offer itself in her mind as an appropriate thing to say, no approach volunteered itself to the woman as one that could be taken to relieve the tension and clarify why the girl was sailing alone and whether she had indeed been sent to retrieve herself and Shadow. Finally, under the unbearable weight of the silence that hushed both the breeze and the flames' crackling, she could no longer stand to look down at the girl's flowing black hair, and faltered, "Hello." Quite to the woman's surprise, this did not in any way assuage the density of the atmosphere, and in fact the silence darkened and deepened after letting her greeting be born into the air, as the girl sat as she had done, still, and seeming very much alone despite the woman's presence, refusing to acknowledge the woman in any way. Once again she tried: "We're, uh…stranded, are you…here to take us home?" she said, instantly regretting her reference to 'home' in fear of her indicating that she knew anything about her shadowy companion's living arrangements, and also the childish way that her words fell from her mouth into the girl's small ears. Still no answer from the girl. The woman, growing braver, walked down the few steps to the lower level, and tried to peer into the silent face to find any unguarded scraps of expression. All she got was a closer view of what she had observed before – that disconnection between mind and body, the intent stare at the bottom of the boat that seemed possible, if continued, to be able to drill a hole through the resilient material that withstood so much unbridled fury from the fires, and open up a portal through which she could disappear entirely. Yet there was no fire in those eyes – they held, in all their darkness, an entirely polar opposite property, a coldness, a desolate, harrowing bleakness, that was so separate from this world that its very mystery made it strangely threatening. It was pain, pure and simple, frozen, wailing pain, that could not allow tears because it was too, too cold to permit weakness. They would be, if permitted to gather, simply turned to ice in the fierce tempest of misery that lived in her eyes. And they were almost hidden completely, underneath those weary lids, but not from that woman at that moment, and like glimpsing the ultimate truth of the world, life and everything, emotion became trapped in her throat, and lodged itself there, refusing to be swallowed. She was overpowered by the sight of that girl, by the sight of her sorrow, of all the sorrow in the world that had not existed to her until recently, and she could not deal with it, she had no means to - she felt that she should look away, but still her gaze remained on that girl, who let the innocent breeze fondle her hair in such a delicate way, and looked as if she would remain there, uncaring and unmoving even if a storm should cast itself upon her, or the fires leap to devour her and all her profound despair.

All at once those dark eyes flashed up at her, and bore into the woman's soul: and from her lips, the words, "My name is Clarity."

8

Glass surrounded her. She could not understand where she was, but as she sat there, her head fixed looking upwards, she seemed to sense that she was inside some sort of a glass box. Light, from an unascertainable source, came bounding towards her, refracting madly to create a blinding mass around her that was so much more offensive to the

eyes than darkness. It would have been easier to accustom the eyes to if
the rainbows and piercing white light fixed themselves in one pattern, but
it seemed the light source was constantly moving, allowing the light
beams to keep playing their manic games with her pained eyes. Fading
into her awareness, as if her ears had just been born into a world of
sound, there came a deep buzzing, low and continuous, and also a faint
whining, the voice of pain waking in the air. Yet it did not sound like a
plea for assistance, and as the sobbing and whimpers continued, and rose
in volume, and continued rising, they seemed to do so without the
knowledge that they were being heard by other ears. The woman,
perplexed as she was by both the visual punishment of the scattering
rainbows of pain to which she could not, for some reason, block out by
closing her eyes, seemed to identify the cries as coming from a man – she
found, as it grew more distressed and more urgent that she could not, like
the light, in any way distract herself from the audio torture either. As she
went to speak, she felt a grip on her throat, a metallic coldness that kept
her voicebox from performing its task, and her mouth flapped about
inanely.

Into this strange, tormenting concoction of sensory saturation,
came another voice, but a voice that was so much more than an auditory
experience – it brought with it a coolness, a calming breeze that swept
over the woman's crouched and cramped body. She did not even seem to
be using words, but it was there, undoubtedly, a soothing presence that
glided like a sweet darkness through the escalating noise of shrieks,
screams and buzzing, and light, light, light that paralysed the eyes and
bore into the mind to wipe out thoughts and obliterate the self into the
overwhelming existence of light. And the woman knew, as she clung onto
that voice, that remained constant while the light and the sound loomed
over her like a growing beast that wanted to consume her and turn her
into the illuminated broken, that this voice was remarkable, it was angelic
and beautiful, it was the sanctuary of all men and all women, it was the
garden itself, a pure, dark night into which she glimpsed an eternity of
salvation from abuse and misery, the peace and liquid freedom into which
only the chosen could melt and allow themselves to become part of that
heavenly darkness. She reached out for it, although she could not move,
she held onto that song without words, those rich and lovely tones that
hid beneath them a black mystery and as she did so, she felt her limbs
stretch out, and the glass box that caged her did likewise, opening wider
to encase her expanding form: she felt her scrunched up body unfold: she
had, in having her body brought into a ball in such restricted
circumstances, and by the way of releasing herself from those
confinements, been physically reborn, and the body that now stretched

out before her was a new one that replaced the previous, worn chrysalis that was no longer of any use. That lovely voice, that voice that was beauty itself, and to which all those wishing to embody such a quality had to copy in weaker forms to ever be seen as coming close to even being slightly pretty, sung over this new body, this new form that tingled at every inch with the dark blessing. The woman came so close to bringing about the bliss of closing her eyes as she moved her body by inches that lay on the fiery heat of her glass cage: her new wings unfurled such alluring colours, a phoenix born in the torrid light that seemed to set the glass on fire with its twisting rainbows and hot, hot beams – the song wound its way above, below, through and around her new skin, and touched that newborn skin with a breath so tender and so cool, dressing her in darkness, teasing at satisfaction. And she was glad that she had not managed the feat of fully closing those eyes that seemed to have been plagued so long now with the invasion of stark light, for above her, the seeds of darkness were laid, and through the blinding light came unmistakably the image of a dark face, and although the woman's eyes were so used now to the assault of light on her retinas, and she could see little else other than the blotches it had left, she felt, if not directly saw, that it was a face, a face that grew larger as it came closer to the lid of the glass box. Heaven is peering in, she thought, heaven is above me looking down on me, pitying me in all its dark splendour and sublime excellence. Then from up there, from the world of incandescence which existed all around her glass box and the light that passed through the barrier between the two as if there was no such barrier in place that prevented the woman from leaving the glass prison, from up there, a dark arm wiped away so much of the light, it grew bigger alongside the darkness of the face, it cast a shadow of cool, refreshing relief onto the hot flesh below, it became larger and larger still, until it seemed it was resting on where the woman perceived the lid of the box to be. And then, if ever anyone had ever been unready for anything in the history of the world and all the lives that had lived therein, the lid was opened, and a colossal rush of noise charged at her ears, an explosion of sound that attacked her mind, for near her - it seemed to be inside her own head it was so near and so loud - a thousand million men were crying for their lives, were screaming and dying a thousand million deaths, were making a thousand million pleas and prayers to gods unknown, were swearing on a thousand million torturers and were choking on blood that spurted from a thousand million dying hearts, and all amongst this, there was an unholy thunder of buzzing that tried to slice at the mind through the ears. The woman gasped at the horror of it all, a huge inhalation that arched her back in its shock, her eyes open more than ever to the dark being that peered now ever closer in hope of finding refuge in the promise of an everlasting cool night, and lay there powerless to the environment around her. One dark finger stood independent of the light, and reached down into the glass pit and met with her burning body – the smooth touch of cold tenderness, its shadows and whispers making their homes upon her skin, licking cool lakes into the hearts of the flames that had sizzled her open pores, a tingling stream of perfection that massaged life into her skin, that made her feel the ultimate feelings that were possible of her body, of all blessed and afflicted with the human condition: all was cool, and open, and singing, and licking, and feeling, and breathing. All was bliss. A night had come to devour her, and it took all of her, her new, untouched form, in a blackness that sighed over her body that was so unaware of the ecstasy of sensation, and it took all of her, and she learned the extent to which rapture could take her, and she let down her guard, and let rapture explore every inch of her that was able to feel, and as it did, she knew well that she was being taken and let it take all of her.

Her gasps and moans finally escaped into the air, and her eyes opened to see that all was black around her. The euphoria drained away, like shadows into the walls as she turned on the lamp, and all that was left was sweat and confusion.

9

The woman turned from the kitchen side back to the sofa and chairs, where her brother had sprawled himself. He already had a drunken air about him, and his gesticulations, which accompanied every utterance that slobbered from his mouth were becoming more and more wild and nonsensical. She set his drink on the coffee table before him and sat down in one of the seats one of his flailing limbs was not occupying, and returned to their previous topic of conversation. "So…when is he coming again?" she ventured quietly, lifting her own glass to her lips and letting it hover to conceal her expression.

"Didn't I tell you darling? It'll only be a few minutes now."

"And…why is he coming?"

Smoke looked at her reproachfully. "Darling, you can't coop yourself up all your life."

"But I'm only-"

"You need to meet more people."

Quiet cast itself over her like a shadow again. "What if- what if he doesn't like me?"

He just smiled and stretched his arms out further over the top of the sofa and pressed the side of his face into his shoulder. A mischievous smile.

"Are you...you sure you haven't had too much already Smokey? Maybe you should pace yourself more."

"Dear sister, dear, dear sister...and Bacchus told all the villagers they could be free for one night, a night of ecstasy, love and wine..."

"I think you have, Smokey, let me get you some water."

That moment the doorbell rang. The woman leaped up instantly, and nervously went to the door, clutching at her sleeve and looking back with worry at her brother. She opened it to a young, conventionally handsome man, who was dressed in scuffed black shoes, tight jeans, a grey top poking through a white shirt and a smart black hat which sat atop tamed blonde hair. His smile was wrought with embarrassment as he faltered, "Is Smoke here?"

"Come in! Come in Minuet," Smoke called, out of view to Minuet, a high pitched drunken voice that bypassed the need for the woman to say anything. She attempted a polite smile and looked down at his shoes as she let him past into the room. Looking out into the hallway she sighed, and gently closed the door.

The evening passed, surprisingly to the woman at least, without much cause for distress or further embarrassment; after the alcohol had pacified the initial nerves, the three found themselves in a comfortable pattern of conversation that roamed freely and steadily through a range of inoffensive topics. Minuet proved to be one of Smoke's shyer friends, but his mind was liberated gradually, and his conversation, although tentative at times, proved to be engaging, so much so that the woman found herself warming to him and even chuckling at a few of his more amusing interjections. As so happens in such circumstances, they stayed up talking and listening to music until the injections of alcohol could no longer stall the inevitable desire to lay one's head on a soft pillow and close one's eyes to rest. They came to such a conclusion and admitted that they had seen the better part of the night as the woman and Minuet noticed Smoke had drifted quietly asleep. The woman chuckled.

"He talks so big yet he can't deny he's human," she said, grinning at Minuet as she drained her last glass of its contents.

"Maybe it was the sheer weight of all those ideas in his head that meant he couldn't keep it up."

"More likely to be the drink."

"You've seen him...how he gets right?"

She sighed. "It's quite a transformation isn't it?"

He laughed and shook his head. The woman presumed that he probably knew more of it than she did. "He staying here tonight, yeah?" Minuet said.

"Yeah. Well, I'm not moving him anywhere that's for sure."

"Alright," he replied, rising from his seat, handing his glass to the woman and making his way to the door. "Thanks for tonight, it was really nice. Smoke was right about you."

She leant her head to the side. She opened her mouth to speak, but closed it again, and just laughed. "I won't ask."

He smirked and looked at the floor. "It was all good, don't worry."

She smiled back at him and held onto the door once he had passed through it. "I'll...well. It'd be nice to do this again sometime," she said, almost wincing as she repeated every word of a well-worn cliché.

"I'd like that," he said. He dug his hands into the back pockets of his jeans. "Well, good night."

"Good night."

She watched him walk a few paces before shutting the door slowly. She remained looking at it for a moment, collecting and trying to understand her thoughts, then turned round to be confronted by the sight of Smoke staring at her full in the face.

"Gosh Smokey. Sorry I woke you up."

His eyes narrowed. "I wasn't asleep."

She gulped. "Oh..."

Smoke shook his head. For some reason he seemed frustrated. "What was *that* about?"

"What?" she asked, timidly.

"Sending him off?"

A sigh of relief. Now she was just confused – too confused, in fact, to craft a reply.

"You hit it off tonight, you two."

"You think so?" The woman was now gathering together the empty glasses and bottles in an effort to dissolve the confrontation into which the conversation was fast hurtling.

"Look, darling, I can't hold your hand every step of the way. I brought him here, acted as a mediator to negotiate a bond between the two of you, but that is the limit, my dear: to think, to hang on to you, to be your mouth piece always, a third party in a relationship! I'm afraid I cannot abide that notion, darling, you just need to pull yourself together and grow up. Live your own romantic life." Quiet descended on the room. He looked back at her to see her staring into the bottom of a glass. "Tough love, darling."

Smoke's eyes stayed on her still figure for some time before finding contentment elsewhere. At length she gathered herself together to continue washing out the glasses, and as she poured water into each one, she watched how it intermingled with the remnants of the alcohol and mixer: her mind could only wander helplessly through thoughts about how individually, the liquids were their own unique entities, yet washed in together, became one black mess, which retained neither the pleasing aroma of the spirit nor the purity of the water. Each could not be seen, nor separated into their original forms. After becoming conscious that she had been gently shaking the glass for some minutes, the woman tipped it up and let the mixture run freely down the sink. That not being enough for her, she shook the upturned glass a little more violently, up and down in the air, to get the last drops out, up and down, up and down, increasingly into a fit of motion, a convulsion of movement that grew in its ferocity, to the extent that Smoke was disturbed from his effort to genuinely fall asleep on the sofa and sat up to determine what exactly was going on. She let out a shriek, further proof to Smoke that she had completely taken leave of her senses, and was about to speak when she slammed the glass down into the base of the sink with such vehemence that it shattered in her hand. Turning, she ran through the room and out the door, leaving Smoke to consider the shattered pieces of glass and the tiny molecules of moisture that dripped from the pointed shards.

The woman ran crazed down the hallway, turning down corridors frantically as if her mind had retreated from her body and was now in hiding, or the logic function in her had somehow been turned off by complete accident. Not a single conscious thought crossed her mind – she did not know what she was doing because it did not occur to her to do consider it, because no thought was able to occur to her mind, a complete blankness enforced itself on her with a fierce impertinence: it was not, as seems to some sometimes, a kind of freeing existence, or a peace that liberated her from the shackles of thought. In a sense, she was liberated, but if she was, it was not in a way that she would have liked, that would appeal to her in her normal, sane, considered mind.

She skidded to a halt as she came round a corner and saw him. In large, determined steps, she made her way towards him – he was walking away from her – and tapped him on the shoulder. As he turned around, he felt her hands grasp his face, and her lips on his: and while she closed her eyes, Minuet's eyes stayed opened until she released him with utter shock and surprise.

10

A cool breeze hummed in the air. It was one of those nights that was so still, and held within the rich darkness a silence that was morbidly eerie and so entirely unnatural that it made solitary wanderers feel that they were the only people to exist in the whole world – that nothing had been, or was, or ever could be, than them, and this black capsule of a night that they inhabited. It was a feeling felt, at least, by a woman dressed in a long black woollen coat, the hood drawn so far over her head that she barely allowed her eyes the privilege of gazing out at the scenery below. She leant on the stone partition with her elbows on the upper walkway of the great wall, and had done for several hours now, watching the sun fade into the sky and the moon emerge to take its throne above her. Or rather, she had been present while sunset had taken a place, but what she was watching for the majority of its duration, no one could say.

She had become insular within the last few days, or weeks, or whatever it had been now - time passed and it seemed she had relinquished so many of her senses recently, and one of those had been her perception of time. Moments when she had lost control of herself haunted her, a constant pain that kept surfacing, a ghost ship that would not sink and kept reaching its skeletal hand up to terrorise again. Her mind felt as if it was matted, as if her hair had receded back into her head and was filling it completely, with knots so vicious that the entirety of her mind had become a heavy tangled mass, and there she was, in the middle of it, looking at it all and screaming. Not knowing where to start. She could not pick at any of it or try to unravel anything, because it was all so ghastly and repulsive and shameful and inexcusable that she could not examine anything that had happened for more than a few seconds before retreating, trying to close her eyes and forget, forget, forget. Maybe if she didn't think about it for long enough she would repress it, she thought, but this was hardly an attainable solution when the act of trying not to think about something always allowed it to return, a sly customer that sidled up to tap her on the shoulder to remind her how much she should feel disgusted in herself. Try harder, she thought to herself, a rare authoritative direct thought that rippled across the black lake of her consciousness and tried to appeal to the other, less controllable levels of her mind to cooperate with the general aim of trying to make her feel better about being who she was and whatever she had done. Yet she had fought this battle every hour of every day that had passed recently, and nothing was happening: if anything the unforgivable memories were penetrating her mind more successfully, were becoming harder to bury, and the traffic in her mind seemed to have been getting worse, a loud, scratching, frantic cacophony of torturous self-deprecation. She stood there, very much alone and unobserved, the wind kicking up around her in various levels of ferocity in a brittle, bitter, biting coldness that numbed the skin and froze the muscles, whilst below her a pit of fire raged and screamed in rebellion at the cold that could never pacify its heat. Yet while it seemed everything else in the world moved, and changed, and aged, the woman stood there, as if her silence and stillness could defy time: the birds above her, and the moon above the birds, and even the sun above the moon, as they looked down, could only gaze upon two things in the world that were defined by such profound and deadening inertia, one of which was made of stone. She felt, in the cold air of winter that whispered death into the ears of the weak, as if she too had been turned to stone, never moving, never changing, never ageing.

She had, consciously or not, been gazing at the dock that she had frequented so many evenings now with the elusive Shadow. All of that business, how it seemed not to matter anymore: it seemed odd to the woman but she had somehow come to accept it all, and even more than that, not even care about the enigma into which she had so inexplicably stumbled. And while she was not caring about that, it seemed trivial that she should care anymore about the other frivolous trivialities that constituted her life: it occurred to her this issue of trying to deduce the mystery of Shadow and the bizarre secrets that orbited that being under black cloth was in a way one of the things that had been propelling her through each day, causing her always to look forward to the next event and to busy herself while she was in the stagnant time between: what had happened in the last few days was that she felt that slip away, she completely lost interest, and consequently, she had completely lost momentum. Momentum. That was entirely it: there was nothing moving her forwards, no pleasures or promises to thrust her into the future, she was stuck, it seemed permanently, somewhere between the past and the present. It was an existence that she inhabited alone, and indeed it was defined by such terms, for two people could not become stuck in one person's head: for although it seemed the world had entirely stopped, it was only the woman's consciousness that had done anything of the sort, and she simply looked at the world with stopped eyes, which prevented her from seeing any movement at all. And yet in her stillness, which seemed to be so still and so quiescent that even thought seemed too violent a disturbance, there was an unspoken part of her that longed for someone to walk into her frozen bubble and share the feeling with her.

The fires still raged below her. The wind still passed its gentle hand over her cheek and then was swept away, and the air was still again. A bird flew through the air, a black dot that could be seen against the milky whiteness of the moon, like a pupil. The towers stood tall, seeming as they always did to be looking down without eyes to the burning cauldron that they stood in timelessly. Without the reminder of a ticking clock, the world lay motionless, a body unconscious. All was still in the dock, the little boats lined up side by side, promising with their very existence between land and sea that more trips would be taken, that another day would dawn, and people would wake again from their slumbers to carry on their lives, having only sustained a slight pause to the continuum of their lives by closing their eyes and lying upon a soft horizontal surface for a certain amount of hours, that light would shine upon these horrid, cold, heartless stones and make them seem less unfriendly as they did at present, that people would meet each other, and laugh, and smile, and shake each other's hands for a triumph or achievement that may happen, that joy could exist sometime in the future for some people some of the time, that once the sun returned then its warm rays would touch the hearts of young and old alike, that the newest, purest toes and the most wrinkled, aged fingers would once again engage themselves for the purpose of living, that people would get on with the business of working, that although hanging their heads in their most private and intimate moments they would, at some point, look up and catch someone's eye, and smile again, and feel happy, even for that split second of their day, even if it was to fade away and be subsumed yet again in the monotony of living, that after even all that was done, and the sun had slid its smiling arch through the sky there would come another night, but one that would feel shorter than this one, that would be over in a blink of an eye, and there it would be again, another day in which all of those glorious things that make life worth living would happen again, to different people, and give them the hope and happiness they needed to forget their troubles and subsequently pass the hours without thought of how the time was shifted, and written in the stories of their lives, and after that, even after all that, there would be another night, and another day, and another night, and the process would continue, and all the people would get through it, they would find their way through this repeating process, the cycle of existing that meant they could experience emotions and moments of varying intensities and be satisfied that that was what was offered to them as people, as beings, and that they were quite content to continue doing so until at a time predetermined by no one that that would all be taken away from them, and then they would feel nothing, and be nothing, and be unable to do anything anymore, they would simply be gone from the world they had come to know and the rules they had come to abide by. All the world, everything around her, seemed to suggest that this was the way the world worked, and would continue to work, but it felt like an eternity away from the permanent minute she inhabited there, standing alone on the great wall, a speck of dirt on the flowing quilt of life.

As permanent as such moments seem, with its paralysis of the mind and body and the tipping of sanity to a place that can never truly be explained with any success by the most eloquent of mortal beings, they do come to an end, and it did end for that woman staring so devoid of feeling and meaning through the darkness that night, in a way that she could not have anticipated, in a way that seemed from her point of view to be an impossible potential case of events. In having fallen into such a stupor that had eclipsed mind and body, she had failed to notice one of those little boats – that looked from her perspective to be miniature toys that floated atop a child's scolding bath – leave the peaceful dock, and the woman's eyes, having been glazed over now for so long that her focus had retreated back into the depths of her mind and saw visual depictions of her thoughts instead of the physical reality that it appeared that she looked on, had failed to trace its slow journey around the backs of the towers. For whatever reason that will forever remain unknown, its return to the dock woke the woman from her incapacitated state – she blinked, drinking in the strange sight, and it took a few minutes for the images to join with the twin prongs of comprehension and interpretation, but eventually, they did converge, and the woman looked down with her mouth slowly opening in shock. Her muscles, that had been condemned to inactivity, to dwindle, and to die, in the woman's apparent unmoving journey into eternal preservation of her standing physical form, found movement again with ease, as if there were never any doubts that the woman would resume her normal life, of moving, of breathing, of changing and aging. Her legs pumped up and down as she clattered down flight after flight of stairs, and ran through corridors, her feet pounding on the floors hungrily, enjoying the buzz of motion again, exhilarated by the whoosh of air past them. Thoughts seeped through again, the flood gates slowly creaked open, and an old familiar feeling whispered through her body, and it was a revelation to her that she was alive, she was living, and could do all the things that living people do – like running. Despite this, only one word took up the majority of her mental space, printed in huge letters in a space that seemed to be just behind her eyes: and that word was Clarity.

She had to pause for breath at one point – another comforting sign that she had regained her place amongst the never-ending line of humanity – on a landing connecting two flights of stairs, and from which, she remembered now, it was possible to see through the window onto the dock that was now only three floors down. She had come so far, but despite her bursts of energy – the likes of which were unprecedented – that had got her to where she was now so swiftly, the entire twenty floors could not be shifted within a short period of time, and as she hobbled, gasping for air and clutching her stomach, to the window, she felt that realistically she could not expect to see the same scene that she had observed from the very top of the great wall, she could not expect that it was moving at entirely different time scale to the one she was working on, and indeed, as she looked down, Clarity was nowhere to be seen. Her desperation at the idea that she could have let her out of her sight once again shot onto her face, she was distraught, yet it was a like a punch in the stomach that only made her more determined to fight the pain and press forwards, and again she went, taking the stairs down, down, down, wishing only that she could detach herself from the ground far enough so that she could simply take one flight of stairs in a single jump from top step to bottom step. Downwards she went, her breaths leaving warmth in the air, a trail of heat from the highest to the lowest point inside that great wall.

The cold hit her in the face, yet not as cold or with as much force that she would have liked to chill her flushed and throbbing skin. The dock was empty. She scanned it several times, as if the girl she chased was so mysterious that she could simply appear out of the darkness without the confinements of a permanent, visible physical body. She wasn't there, it had to be admitted, and she turned back to the building, her feet poised to run again, once they received a report as to which way they should do so. Mixed orders came, they turned this way, then that, then turned another and were set in motion again – up stairs – along corridors – back the corridor – through some doors – up the stairs – along another corridor. She stood at a point where two corridors converged with the one she had just come down, in a Y shape, and stared: in one, in the distance, she could see the approaching figure of Smoke, his arms swinging audaciously by his sides, she turned, panicked, and down the other there was a crowd of people, containing everyone she had ever worked with - almost it seemed, everyone she had ever known - and with increasing terror she looked down the only way left remaining, to see Minuet speaking with someone at the door to a unit, looking as if he was about to turn her way, and soon spot her, and see her so possessed in her feverish hysteria that she could not explain and did not want to explain and could not even explain to herself: looking, crazed, around herself for some sort of safe place, a sanctuary where she could hide, and be healed, and find normality in her own time, and reclaim her senses once more, she grabbed a door at complete random, tried the handle, and when it opened, flung herself inside, and closed it, forcing her back against it so that no one could get to her.

There was only darkness. Once her insane heart beats had slowed, so that it no longer sounded like her head was being perpetually banged against a wall, her sharp, panicked breaths filled the room with sound. She listened to herself breathing, dispassionately, as if listening to another person breathing, and began to wonder what it was that distressed the breather so. Then she began to wonder where she was, and what in fact, she was actually doing. Had she a plan? It seemed, from the way her life was weaving, silly to be under the pretence that she ever was, or ever could be; there were so many unexpected and unfathomable forces that exerted far more control than she had on her life, it seemed ridiculous to feel that she was in control of any part of it. She felt herself jump out of her skin as in the darkness, a match was struck, and a flame flickered timidly not far from her. She could see very little surrounding it, only an arm and a hand that held a candle that it sat on top of, like a burning hat. Yet, somehow, she was not scared. She waited for the feeling to come, but as the light came nearer, she stood blank and simply looked into the darkness, into where she expected this presence to be. The figure and the flame separated themselves from each other; the candle being set upon a surface at about hip height. She heard a sashaying of clothes as the presence came closer to her. A girl, about her height, was slowly materialising into her awareness, so slowly, and in such small degrees, and as her eyes became accustomed to the level of light, she could make her out, she could see this girl emerging like a heavenly body from the darkness, her eyes trained exactly to meet the woman's, as if she had a secret way of seeing through blackness - there was such a profound intensity in her eyes, and her body, and in everything about her, an aura, a *something* of calmness, that flowed like waves over the woman, who relaxed her grip on the handle of the door and let her hand slowly fall beside her, and watched as if her entire existence was only eyes, the girl came closer to her, not an arm's length now she was, looking deep into her eyes, she could feel her breath now, she could see into her eyes deeper now, they were breathing as one now, she was still moving, closer now, closer, so much closer, and still the breathing, it got deeper and fuller, it was a huge effort now, her shoulders moving up and down with the breath, and she could feel the sweet air of the girl's on her own cheeks, and feel the tingling in the stomach as she was breathing heavier, heavier, anticipation for the moment when their worlds would collide, and still the girl was emerging from the darkness, she could see the dark brown swirl of her eyes, she could see nothing else, be nothing else apart from the eyes and the breath and the pulsating of her body and the heat of the skin, two beings burning alone in the darkness that was the great unknown, an endless black night nothingness that was there before the world was made, and this moment of two beings coming close now, their colliding in the next minute, any second now, was the creation of the world as it had come to be, there was nothing else that existed in the world apart from the black void and these two souls, the woman, and the girl, breathing in unison, their eyes together as one, gazing into each other's minds, with no barriers, nothing saved and nothing hidden, gazing into each other and anticipating the creation of the world.

Don't let the darkness come, Clarity, don't let it go dark again, let me enjoy this, let me enjoy you, if even for a minute, you are my only relief, my only promise of joy – let me have this…

Let me have you

Barely lit as they were, their faces occupying the same air, breathing the same air, living in the same place, for that moment living the same life, they slid to meet each other in mirroring movements – the touch the most delicate, the most soft and sensuous, as they met each other for the first time, and while their mouths parted they held out their hands to each other, as if they did not need to see, their eyes were simply superfluous, aesthetic components of the human form, and so they closed their eyes as if they never need open them again, because they sensed each other, flowed through each other's skin with sensations of bliss and hunger and reassurance, they became each other's skin, a case that held within them such animals, that longed to play, and tumble, and fight, and within them, their lonely hearts that were so gentle, and pure, and full of such utterly profound and poisonously tragic longing…

You opened the box, Clarity, you opened the box

She felt her face against the girl's stomach, against her cool, dark skin, and she felt a hand explore its way through her light, free hair, and as it did, and as she was held with such kindness and protection against the soft, soft skin, she felt a tear fall from her eye and roll down to come between the two of them, then mould them together in that salty liquid.

You opened the box

11

I can't begin to explain. There's just something – have you ever felt that the world was conspiring against you – and it got bigger, it just got so big, it was colossal, and I thought I had control of it, I thought I could contain it and it would be mine, my little thing, a secret I suppose, that would be mine, my little world where I could control all the protagonists like puppets, and it would all go how I wanted it to go, the story would unravel in such a beautiful way, because, I don't know, I believed that I had the power to control people, I thought I could be the pane of glass between them and the world, that every now and then I would tilt and show things not quite how they really were, but how I wanted them to seem, so that people would then think of things in a different way, and everything I told them would be framed in such a way that it would make obvious to them the course of action that they should take, and they would think it was their idea, and be happy that they thought of it and I would agree, and that would make them feel like they were their own person, and really all of it was just playing into my hands like a dream – I would be the puppet master extraordinaire – and for a while it did work. The first thing happened and I thought I can make something of this, I can leap from obscurity and make something of it. Oh but now – but now...I know I've got out my depth, I know, I know, because now it's all happening around me, *I'm* the puppet, and I'm at the bottom of the glass and they're all around the sides staring down on me, I've sunk downwards so low so so low that I can barely see them, but their faces are still there I know, looking down and laughing and judging – why did I never think they had their own minds? How could I be so foolish, so sure of myself – but really, you know, the world is not simple, I used to know someone, he said to me the world is so simple, you know, and it's simple because everyone makes it seem so complicated, but I know now he was wrong, this is not a simple world because it fucks you around, oh my darling I have never felt so low in all my life, and they never tell you about it, they never say a goddamn word maybe because they don't want to see the spark in your eyes get dimmer, and fade away, but that is what happens anyway, why couldn't anyone tell me, why doesn't anyone help me, why do they all look down on me as if they can't see themselves in me, they can't see the way that this feeling tears me apart and is actually tearing them apart inside too, they look at me as if I'm not human but I am, they just can't admit it to themselves and maybe that's the difference between us, but in you, I saw it in you, and I just couldn't move away from you, I just couldn't let you go knowing that you share something with me, that we've been joined together in this way because we were the only ones that would admit it to ourselves, and I don't know what I wanted to do with it and with this recognition that we mirrored in each other, all I knew was that I needed to be near you, and I felt ashamed of myself, so ashamed, god it haunted me night and day this feeling but it felt so much better to admit it to myself, and to you, and it cracks me up inside because I think you're not even real, you seem to be so magical that I can't even believe it when I touch you, it is completely a dream and it feels like it would kill me to believe in you but there's nothing else I can do because I need you, I need you because I need

relief

that is the only thing that I need it just all is on top of me, all around me, this terrible feeling and I can't let it go, you are what I need, relief, relief, relief, from the horrible twists and turns of this world this life and I don't even know if you can give it to me, I don't know if you can even hear these words that I am forming now, I don't even know if you can even see me and see all this distress that is stuck inside of me and emerges on the surface of my face, I don't know, but I don't care, life doesn't mean a goddamn thing and you are the only thing that can make me feel otherwise because you have it in you too this parasite this feeling is inside you like it's inside me and that bonds us, can't you feel it, how together we are in this moment and every moment that we feel desperate, that inside that sinking feeling there is a hand reaching down, not to pull me up and take me back to the surface, but a hand, a desperate hand that is sinking with me, and together we are devoured by the bog, the marsh, the sinking sand, whatever yours is, don't you feel that? Oh god, don't answer, don't answer, I couldn't bear to be wrong, I couldn't bear for you to tell me that I'm not real, or that you're not, or that only misery in life is real, because what would all of us be doing here – would I go back, would I stop now and start back at the beginning simple and unaware with no truth, no idea about the truth inside me, would I, would I, I don't know you tell me, can't I stop it, all I want is to touch you again, you fill me with the most agonising sweetness, the most bitter and blissful sensation, a bite on the tongue that lets the sugary blood flow into my mouth, why all of a sudden have I become so weak, become this person that seems so far away from the start, the beginning, how have I changed and what is it that changes us, the harsh realities of life, is it life that changes us because we are nothing other than our lives, I don't know, all

I know is that I want it to stop, stop, stop all I want is to know and to feel the silence of

relief

all I see in my mind is a list of Is a list of me all about me I don't want it to be just words sandwiched between I and me that mean nothing, just a venting of the mind within but it is just so phenomenal, it is just so huge that it rips at my very fibres, it oozes out of my seams, the words are escaping from my joints, from in between my toes there comes a description of my desperation, and out of my elbow comes a call for salvation, there is just *no way* I could keep this inside any longer it's just too big, my skin is not big enough to contain it anymore and I have to let you know even though I know it's inside you too how can you lie there and not say a word I don't know but all of your heavy silence is like a gift to me, I don't know how you can keep it inside because this is bigger than me, I cannot contain, and I see it in your eyes, I see everything in your eyes, I suppose that's how you let it out, you let it out to me, I feel everything, in an instant I know everything, you don't need to say a word, I know how much you suffer but is it so much that we can't create something positive is it sacrilege to say such a thing please forgive me I am nothing don't let me disappear don't fade away and stop being real because you are the realest thing to me the most tangible existence I have is in you and you might not even be here and still all of this you know is just too much for me relief relief relief is what I need and you are that to me could I ever even imagine what I am to you please don't please don't move your lips again don't say a thing you don't need to don't even think about saying a word.

12

A s she bent down, her hand squeezed the sponge over the bucket, and the grey water spilled through her fingers and left little specks of dirt all over her skin and underneath her fingernails. She submerged the sponge in the grimy water once again, allowing it to grow with the absorption of the liquid, and rose to stand. The sponge was set in motion on the grey, cold surface on the wall, and as it slid in slow, overlapping circles, stagnant drops traced their weary journey downwards towards the cold stones. As she moved, the woman's bare feet were dampened by those excess drops, and intensified the cold that she already felt, sending a shiver from the very base of her up through her limbs and outwards over all of her skin. She cleaned, and continued cleaning, although now there was a fatigue in the movements that were no longer smooth and caring – her bones moving like fast ageing clockwork, moving forwards and backwards in a run down manner, as if at any moment she would stop entirely. Maybe it was the cold that made her feel like she should stop, take a break, and come back to the task refreshed, or maybe because it was such a routine action that the act itself was infiltrating her muscles, creating tension and speeding up the process of decline and decay to the degree where even the slightest movement sent spasms of pain all along her arm: either way it was hard to discern, but regardless she continued in her efforts. She did not turn, nor stop, nor barely notice when the door behind her creaked loudly open, a person slipped into the room, and carefully replaced the door to its closed form. Little notice was paid at all to the disturbance, and the woman's eyes remained fixed on the task being executed.

There was a shifting of feet, a throat being cleared and a sigh. Silence, all but occasional squeaks from the sponge slithering over the surface. Finally. "How are you?"

Silence. Sigh.

"I hope…I hope you're feeling better, dear, I hope you have been at any rate."

Squeak. Another sigh, deep, a slow, slow exhale. The dropping of the shoulders was almost audible.

"Everyone's…well…I just want you to know, I'm here for you. Darling. You know that, right? I wouldn't want you to feel…that I wasn't. I'm w- …here for you, dear, don't let anything tell you otherwise."

She bent down – a hard movement that almost creaked with its pain - to expel the sponge's water into the bucket, then stood up again, and began wiping with the sponge dry.

"I do hope you're feeling better."

Hollow silence, maybe for a minute or so. The sound of a mouth opening, then closing – the slight intake of breath as if words were to follow, and then didn't, for whatever reason.

"I'll…come back, soon. I…"

    Shoes tapped their way over the stones, one after the other, like a grandfather clock counting the seconds. The door whined as it was pulled open, and let out a lower whimper as it was dragged back to its place. Then nothing could be heard apart from the methodical wiping of the grey surface. She looked closer at the surface, having cleaned a small area in the top corner free from grime and dust and noticed that it reflected the hand she held up to it. She drew back her hand then stared at the grime to the side of it, losing her gaze in the complex layers of dirt and the many patterns therein.

The door creaked open once again.

"I.." Sigh. "I love you, darling."

The door whimpered back as it closed.

    The pattern that the woman was following with her eyes weaved in a strange line and she had just found herself back at the clean patch of the mirror, like following a stream to the ocean, in time to see the reflection of the figure that had re-opened the door for a few seconds before the door was closed again. She looked at the reflected door, her head to one side, her eyes barely open with fatigue, and began to move her lips, as if trying to fashion a word in the air, but no sound came out, and no word was created. Gradually, she turned around to face the actual door, saw it was closed, waited moments to see if it would remain so, then turned round again to the grey surface. She stared, for a minute, into the filth, her face devoid of expression. Then she bent down, let the sponge swell with water, stood up, and began to wash the surface in circular motions again.

*

    Her eyes fluttered open like drugged butterflies taking to the air. It was hard for her to separate her eyelids enough to get a clear picture of what lay ahead of her, for the sticky substance that acted like natural glue and obscured her interpretation of the visual world. The picture did not need to be seen however, being a familiar sight and not a welcome one at that: the impulse to open her eyes was more of an unconscious one that accompanied the unwanted sensation of waking that befell her. With that feeling came with it, as is customary, an opening awareness of the room around her, the temperature – which was cold, and seemed to be permanently so – and the air quality – which was always bad, seeming as it did that oxygen had to be hunted rather than presumed to enter the lungs in the normal fashion – as well as the standard of light. Today, like any other day that had come before or any other day that would proceed it, a murky half-light, somewhere between real light, where everything could be visible, and real darkness, where nothing could be seen, reigned over the space. Not a sound could be heard.

She heaved a finger up to her eyes and tried to clear them out so she was able to see. Her face felt wet, a kind of dew that had grown over her frail body that lay uncomforted and sore upon the cold cobbles of the floor. Her hand spread over her face, obscuring her opening eyes, as her mouth tried to open. Her throat was dry, and thirsty. Eventually she dragged her hand down her face so that she could see again. She took it all in: and it was not much, from where she lay, but then again, there was not much that could be seen from any position in this room – her eyes caught the reflection of herself, staring back at her, her light hair dishevelled and saliva dripping from her mouth, her arms around her body and her legs tucked into her stomach. The mirror met the floor, and rose past her standing height, after the woman had lifted it off of its mount – for some reason she had preferred it on the floor, resting against the wall. She blinked, and looked into her own eyes, as if waiting for the other to make the first move. No one made a move, until the woman became sick of staring at herself – she could no longer pretend it was someone else, the person that she saw seemed to fit her so well, to be so like her, that there was little way of distancing herself from her anymore.

At length she got up. She did not know why. She shuffled her way over to the chair, which had only a small cushion that was fraying and threadbare, and the wood seemed to sag slightly, but it took her weight with little complaint. She stared expressionless, in a waking stupor, at the desk that sat with the same tired dreariness that she did. Her hand eventually broke the stillness and reached for the drawer, and proceeded to pull out a piece of paper and a black pen. Her vacant eyes watched without emotion as her hand scrawled ragged letters over the page, with increasing speed and urgency:

MY dearest,

It has been – longer than I thought I could imagine. Do you still remember me? I can understand. I can.

This time without you cannot break me. I will stay true to you in every movement, in every thought in every day.

I know

I know you do not remember me. But I will love you, as I always have.

I always

I am not sure I know. I am not sure I know who you are anymore. Did I ever?

Do I still remember you? Will you understand?

Could I ever call you by your name?

I do not know how to sign my name to you, so forgive me. I shall just be –

Yours ever true

The page was folded in half, then in half again. She stood, her body seeming a little lighter than before, her steps exhibiting more energy, though never quite becoming energetic. She soon found herself at the window, looking down through the dirty pane to the world below. The sun, though hidden between clouds in the sky, was still beaming down enough light to catch the many disturbances in the lake below, which was the only thing that could be seen from the woman's window. A single blue square, in which only the slight movements of the surface made by the wind, rain, fish or on occasion, a boat, could be viewed: this was the woman's entire impression of the outside world. She had spent many times, early on, staring at such a scene, taken in by the tranquillity of the inactivity, the liquidity of the colour, and the calmness of the transparent depths that so starkly contrasted with the fire in her eyes, but now: now she could barely look at it for a second, she could barely overcome her revulsion for long enough to complete the task at hand. She looked down impassively at the paper in her hand. There was a slight gap between the small window and its frame at the very bottom, and it was towards this that her hand now reached towards. Poised, page in the air, and in the last moments before the act was committed she was woken from her concentration on the task: an unintelligible noise at first that rose in volume, but came to sound increasingly like footsteps, taking the stairs towards her current position. Panic flared, a spark inside her that flipped upside down her insides, and her hand trembled as she rocked back and forwards between two opposing courses of action. The page fluttered between withdrawal and banishment. Louder, louder, like knocks on the doors of Hell, like impetuous rings of a knell that scorned at her indecision and threatened discovery, brutal and forever damning discovery. Her eyes wild and afraid, she finally made her compromise: and so, folding the already folded paper in half, then half again, and then yet again, she placed it inside her mouth, and tried to dissolve it in her saliva, to tear it with her teeth, to tempt it down her throat – anything, to make it disappear completely. She dropped to the floor, still shaken inside and very much in fear of the crashing sound of heavy, judging feet that had now risen in her mind to a deafening level, a noise that shook her visibly as it pounded the stones outside and the core of her being. Half led, half sat, in a defensive ball, her eyes looking out like a condemned, confused animal as it beholds the rusted cleaver hovering in the air the second before the violent strike. When it seemed the infernal battering could no longer ascend to a louder volume, and that if it did, then surely the entire room, building and indeed world would immediately fall and become pitiful servants to its almighty power, it stopped. The key was heard in the door, a sickening, screeching, metal on metal cry, and it was pushed violently open.

13

"**D**o you mind if I…?"

The woman's head may only have twitched slightly, but it was enough for her visitor to reach into his coat to pull out his cigarettes and lighter, and to begin puffing away in a way that did not seem to alleviate his stress at all, but rather make it worse. While he looked around, his eyes searching for words to form into a coherent and appropriate sentence, the woman's eyes looked up at him, big and scared, as they had remained for some hours now, never ceasing in their bulging fear and dread of the worst, whatever that might have been. The times that their eyes met were few and far between.

"Has anyone…?" The visitor seemed not to need to finish his questions for some reason, and never required a reply to them either, but simply presumed the woman's probable responses in their interaction, or lack of. "I suppose, yes…yes…" He let the smoke pour from his mouth, a gassy eruption of filth into an atmosphere that already lived in a deadening monochrome world without it. The visitor leant on his knee with his hand and looked intently at his cigarette that he was playing with in his other hand. "Quite the…" He let his mind and mouth run free with

his thoughts and never seemed to dwell entirely in the silent world, nor in
the spoken one. Various false starts and attempts at observations poured
from his mouth, like pollutants to contaminate the ear.

"I guess, that's the…"
"What with the…"

"…will always be…"

"Got to find…" He lit another cigarette after stubbing out his first, and
the alteration between the two states seemed to have, for the moment at
least, broken the strange state that he had lapsed into. The fiddling with
the smoking toy could no longer occupy his unfocused gaze and he
deflated sonorously. He looked at her with tactful caution, his lips tight
and tense and turned slightly inwards, and on catching those frightened,
staring circles, that seemed like blank plates onto which he had to lay the
meal, he looked down at the floor. Quiet exploded into the room, and it
seemed that the smoke wriggling out of the cigarette was almost audible.
The visitor hung his head for quite some time. She looked up as she had
done for some time, devoid of thought or speech.

"She's dead."

A flash of the eyes at her. She still stared back, just the same, no
trace of recognition or comprehension in her expression. A drag on the
cigarette. The smoke poured into the next words.

"She's dead."

He looked up again. Nothing. Just fear. Animal fear. Primal. Not a
clue. He slid a tongue over his lips and maintained eye contact with her.
Harder this time.

"She's dead."

A glaze that could not be permeated. He hung his head, rubbed his
forehead and closed his eyes as he took yet another drag on the cigarette.
He looked up at the ceiling, expelled the grey breath and opened his eyes
again. Another attempt at keeping their eyes together. He tilted his head
downwards, moved closer in, and looked with open, firm eyes, his hand
on his leg and he moved his lips very slowly.

"She is dead."

He lingered for a minute or two, staring into her, but there was nothing. A husk. Only it was a husk filled with fear, but a husk nonetheless. Finally, he could not take the intensity any longer, and pulled himself away from her, and sat back in his chair. He rubbed his hand over his mouth, then stood up, paced for a while, went to the window, stubbed out his cigarette, lit another one, and sat down again. He looked down at her again. His mouth opened, a hand went through his hair. A tear slipped from his eye. Then that was it. The visitor fell to the floor, on his knees, and cried, cried heartily, wept violently, moaned with complete desolation and felt himself to be collapsing entirely under the strain, while the woman, curled into herself, with her big, big open eyes looked on, and could offer nothing but her relentless fear of all around her.

*

The sun was setting. The world outside had grown a darker blue, and soon it would be black entirely, apart from the highlighted rising and falling of ripples that the moon cast her gaze over. The woman had risen from the floor, and was standing quite still in the middle of the room, managing to overpower the weight of the lead atmosphere around her. For whatever reason, bravery had risen from somewhere within her, and she looked with feverish eyes at that square, through the portal to the other side. She stood alone, and cold, and empty, the web of darkness weaving its threads around her, clamping her and making her unknowable in the blackness, in the totality of the void, but still she preferred to stand and watch the liquid blue with a strange and compelling fixation.

And then it happened.
Without warning
Without precedent,

There emerged a boat

How she could ever be sure that it was indeed a boat that momentarily soared into her line of vision, she had no idea, but the image was unmistakable, it was an austere vision of such gravity that her life changed instantly, *she* changed within a second, and her purpose and direction, her thoughts, mood, stance, temperature, senses, emotions, fantasies, dreams, dreads, fears, concepts, memories all altered irrevocably to a state where she had become an other, a different entity than the one she had been before that moment. For on that vessel that had so suddenly and so unapologetically appeared, there had sat, facing her direction, a shadowy figure, a person all in black with a hood drawn far over the face, and another, who sat opposite, someone that the woman only saw as a blur – an unrecognisable back of a head. A slow, dripping sensation began to trouble her stomach, a shadow of cool, thick fear trickled over her skin – a state that she slid into without panic or distress, but that seemed to consume her entirely: and maybe it was more of simply knowing what was to follow this moment in time, more than the fear that it could happen. Whatever it was, the following became clear to her: that within long, she was certain to die, and was certain to do so at the hands of that robed traveller on the boat.

*

"Only in the darkness, only at night Clarity comes."

"We can't keep doing this, you know."

"Oh my love, my love, they could never keep us apart."

"I know my darling. It's just –"

"Ssh, my dear, don't speak anymore, you don't need to, I want to say so much to you, I don't know how I make it through the days, the weeks, without you...all the things they say to me, it's not right, it's not right, all those things they've tried to tell me...promise me you'll keep coming."

"It's getting harder, my dear, I can't deny it –"

"Tell me! Tell me Clarity! Tell me, promise me, you will come again, you won't leave me here, I can't live without you, you *know* that."

"I will always try, my love. You know I will always be inside of you."

"No Clarity! That's not enough. It's really not enough anymore. I need to see you, I need to feel you beside me, you need to be here, otherwise they'll wave their magic wands and they'll tell me you won't come again and I'll start to believe them."

"Come on, my love, they can never take me away from you. You'll always love me. I'll always love you."

"But...I think they're already starting to win."

"My love?"

"I think..."

"Yes?"

"Nothing."

"Come now, talk sense. You love me. I love you. There is nothing else."

"You're right."

"I am the darkness. And I will always follow the day."

"You're right."

"I'll always fade into your arms then dissolve again as the sun rises."

"You're right."

"I am. And so are you."

"You're right."

"And so are they."

"You're…no…Clarity?"

"Yes my love?"

"What was there before me?"

"Nothing."

"Oh."

"What was there before me?"

"Well…lots of things. Pain. Loneliness. No one understood me. I never went out. I never did anything. I was…nothing."

"So the same as me?"

"Yeah…yeah, I guess so. Clarity?"

"Yes my love?"

"I love you."

"I love you too, my love."

"Never leave me."

"I won't."

"Are you sure?"

"Yes."

"Even if they –"

"Even if they. Yes."

"But what if…what will happen?"

"They can't make me leave you. They'll only make you leave me."

"I won't."

"I know. There's no need to worry."

"But why do I?"

"Do you have any doubts?"

"No. I don't know what it is. You know…you know I love you."

"I love you too, my love."

"I want to say more but that is the only thing I can say. There's something more I want to say, but the only way I can say it is by saying those words that I've used so many times to mean different things. You don't think I'm just saying it do you?"

"No, I know you mean it, my love."

"Clarity, when will you come again?"

"I don't know."

"What can I do without you?"

"Don't forget me."

"I couldn't. It's easier to forget me than it is to forget you. There's more of you in me than there is me in me."

"I am only you."

"Clarity, in the day, I'm not right...I don't understand anything anymore. Everything seems so strange. I feel like I can feel the world tilting, and it's going to throw me off. Daylight is so confining. Only at night can I stretch out and feel right again, because I know I'm in your home when it's night time, it's where you live, and sometimes when you do come it is the best thing in the world and I wonder why I ever had any problems. But then you go – I know you have to go – and everything is horrible. Everything is death. And you are my life, Clarity, you are my life."

"You are my life too."

"Clarity?"

"Yes, my love?"

"Is death coming again?"

"Yes my love."

"Clarity?"

"Yes, my love."

"Will you hold me?"

"Yes, my love."

14

Somewhere in the outside world, in the world that the woman could not understand or imagine, a world that she felt by all rights should not exist, a cockerel crowed its alarm call. It was piercing, audacious and unafraid, and it drove sleep away from many that morning; yet the woman could only hear it as a personal attack on her peace, on her few snatched moments of being able to escape conscious perception of the world and its troubles. She threw her damp hand over her face to prevent her eyes from snapping rebelliously open and revealing the same dreary confinements once again. A repeating day that would never change, never progress, never age.

She sat up shivering and staring beyond every object that she looked at. A different dimension had opened up in front of her and she could no longer see those grey stones, that dirty mirror, that unforgiving door – to do so would be to admit the truth of the situation, to admit failure. She thought that she was seeing into forever, into an eternity of moons and planets and stars and supernovas and suns, into the creation of all life, the reason for existence: but all of that powerful knowledge, in trying to squeeze itself into her mind, scraped at the edges and filled her head with cold, metallic pain, and shot out of her eyes as oozing, black oil.

Her shoulders contorted up and down as she sobbed. They continued to as the door swung open and the guard inspected her quarters. He looked down at her, his round, brown eyes solid and defiant as he tried to understand whether he should comfort her or leave her be. She did not look up.

Are you

what

I just

what

well

what

Nothing.

go your own way

I…

you do
don't you

make decisions for yourself

yes

how is it

you let it get this bad?

Me?

yes you

yes

yes you

what has happened

You're very upset

that's not even the start

I

I let myself

I let myself

somewhere along the line

I did too

what can you know

we
all
fall
just some of us land

why do you always
why do you

why do you always look at me

there is nothing in your eyes

just nothing

explain to me what you mean

nothing is certain

only certain is nothing

explain to me what I mean

you mean nothing, I mean nothing,
only there is something in your eyes

do you love me could you ever love me is such a concept completely
foreign to the human race

no

but still you hesitate

I used to think I...
I used to think I was neither attracted to men
Or attracted to women

I was nothing

Someone terrible
That needed to be punished

that faded

why did it fade
when did it fade

a long time ago
things always happen a long time ago
even if it's yesterday

how can you be sure that you are you
and not me

I wanted to be you
I wanted to be you too

Why me?

I could ask you the same.

Fate is cruel

you believe in such a thing?

I believe in a force that is making my life

Hell

Can I help?

you can help me no more than you can help yourself.

I can't do that.

well then
don't offer your services

it's cruel to believe sometimes

      well I do believe

           I have to

what else is there

       for either of us

          is there?

only nothing

    I don't know what's wrong with you

     why are you crying

        I can't help you
        I'm sorry

        I'm sorry

        I'm sorry

oh god it's happening again
        I'm sorry

make it
make it stop   I'm sorry

make it
make it end   I'm sorry

there is just something so fundamental about both of us that needs to be
cured
   I can't help you
      I know.
   I can't help you
      So why do you try?

   I can only watch
      So why do you cry?
   I can only watch
      I know.

      I'm holding the rope

       hold it

or

let

go

I CAN'T HELP YOU

I think my....

I CAN'T FUCKING HELP YOU

grasp

is

JUST DIE THEN

slipping

such startling words for you

my

love

will I be the one who makes you jump?

like to think I've done something useful

you want to see me go

well you'll go

before me

my

love

you will

STOP IT

I want to see your

STOP IT NOW I DON'T WANT TO HEAR IT   blood bubble

THIS IS TOO MUCH   your

I
AM NOT STRONG ENOUGH

brains boil

a clash of cymbals

the rich clotting desire of death

the tournament has begun

you think just because you're going down

you
can
take
me
with

you

you can't

my love

it glides on the wind   you can't

I won't let you leave   I won't let you

I won't let you stay

a breeze choking with sulphur

your life will be mine

I'll walk away with yours

merge with me

merge

how many times do you think

I've wished we could change

places

I've read your words

                              I don't take kindly to that kind of abuse

          oh but you love it darling

                              you want to die I know

          you
                  can't
                          fool
                                me

that's what I saw in your eyes

          nothing   STOP IT

                  it's death   STOP IT RIGHT NOW

                      my dear little boy

who's on the inside here

                      who's on the outside
                                          I'M THE SANE ONE

my little fool
              to have to hold

                      to charm   YOU CAN'T

                      too cold   HAVE

                                                  ME

I'm still free

              You're not

                      You think you are

              But you're not

You are nothing
And everyone knows it

Try living in the real world
You might become real

*

"Clarity?"

"Yes my love."

"Am I real?"

"Yes, my love."

"How can you tell?"

"I can hear you, I can see you, I can touch you, I can do this to you…"

"Maybe you're right."

"Don't you worry that I'm not real?"

"Come now Clarity, don't, you sound like them again."

"But really?"

"I worry that when I wake up you'll be gone. And you are. I worry about reality, and that is real. I don't worry about you because…no I do worry about you…you are real, and it's the reality that's not real…those days, they're not real, because they're painful, the people that come to see me, they're not real, they're enemies, they're agents, they're trying to infiltrate and bring me down, who could believe in them. Am I right Clarity? I feel so confused. Let's not talk about it. You'll always be here won't you Clarity?"

"Yes, my love."

"Even if I-"

"Even if. You should know me by now my love."

"I do know you, Clarity, I do. It should be so simple, with our love, my love for you is simple and I want to be simple for you, Clarity, I just don't seem to be managing it, there's so many thoughts in my head and I can't shift them, I can't order them around. Clarity, you'll always be here, won't you, Clarity, my love, my angel, my darkness?"

"Yes, my love."

"Say something else."

"Yes, my love."

"Come on, Clarity, say something else, please, just tell me anything to break the horrible noises in my head, please, my darling."

"You are my love, and I love you, always, and I won't disappear, I'll always be here, I'll always be here to love you."

"But if I…if I never write another word for you, will you still exist?"

"Yes, my love."

"Because Clarity…I stopped writing today."

"Did you?"

"And I want you to stay around Clarity, don't ever leave, you won't ever leave will you Clarity?"

"I'll never leave you, my love."

"You don't feel any different?"

"No."

"Then neither do I. Clarity, will you do something for me?"

"Yes, my love."

"Will you…will you call me by my name?"

"Why?"

"I just…it's…well. I've never heard you say it. You do know it, don't you?"

"Yes, my love."

"Then why don't you ever use it?"

"I…"

"It's okay. Don't worry Clarity. I remember, I remember when we first met you never used to say anything. I didn't know what you would say, until it become obvious to me the kinds of things you would say, and it was then that you opened your beautiful mouth and let those words pour out in your lovely voice…I felt you, before then, I knew who you were but you didn't have a name and you didn't have a body all you were was a feeling inside me that I needed you, and then I saw you and that was it, there you were, and you became everything to me, you were my exquisite darkness…when will you come back, Clarity?"

"I don't know, my love, it's getting harder-"

"You will always try, won't you Clarity. Try to see me, won't you Clarity, you'll always love and cherish me like no one else has, won't you Clarity, you'll always be my answer, won't you Clarity, you'll always be there to kiss me and make me feel good, make me smile and make me have those special feelings and tell me to put my feet up and make me think of that house we will have one day together and live there together in harmony and one day we'll go outside and holding hands skip down to the river and sit there with fishing rods the dark blue metal of the fishing box at our sides and a picnic hamper that you packed because you're oh so good at those sorts of things and love to look after me and we'll sit there with the wind flowing through the trees and the water beneath us and we'll lean in together and you'll tell me secrets and I'll laugh and we'll both laugh together about how silly things in life are and we'll maybe not catch any fish but we'll sit there all the day in the most blissful kind of sunshine that will sparkle in your eyes and people will walk past on the footpath behind and we'll wave maybe at a few of the children dancing past and with their skipping ropes and they'll all see you in the real light of day and everyone will see how happy we are I mean some of them might be the jealous type they might look on us with scorn and wish that they were in love too but it wouldn't matter to us because we would just be us and that's all that matters isn't it Clarity that we're together and nothing ever takes us apart because you know I couldn't live without you you know it would cut me down and I would fall like a tree in those woods I would fall into that river and my blood would fill up the river and no fish would ever swim there again because I would poison all the water and everything around would die but no we're not going to die are we Clarity we'll live together forever in a wood log cabin open fires and biscuits and mugs of cocoa and slippers and dressing gowns and showers hot hot showers and evenings with the music playing in our ears and we'll be so happy won't we Clarity all of this is real isn't it Clarity this is real we're there now aren't we Clarity in our little wooden bungalow with all the children waving with their skipping ropes how glad they are that we had a picnic and we'll love each other won't we Clarity because you're real and everyone will see you're real and we'll live together forever won't we Clarity because you'll never leave because you're happy with me so so happy with me that you'll never want anyone else but me and I'll never be able to understand it myself when I pour out your cereal on a morning and take it to you in bed with a flower I freshly pick from the garden here's your flower Clarity isn't it lovely doesn't it make you smile to think that there's so much good in the world and nothing is ever bad there is no bad and everyone is lovely and nothing is bad and everyone loves each other but none like mine and Clarity's never have to cry for anything will you my beautiful never a tear to soil your tender cheeks that have seen so much pain already…isn't that…isn't that right Clarity, that we'll…we'll live together and we'll…love each other to show the world the right way…to love…the way that has never been loved…before…in   this   world…isn't   that…isn't   that…isn't   that right…Clarity…?"

"Yes, my love."

15

The woman laid on the cold floor in the dark, drifting in and out sleep. She had not dreamt now for a long time, and although she tried to conjure up pleasing thoughts and scenarios in her mind, so that she might visit them in her dreams, she found this to be entirely fruitless, but nevertheless kept pursuing the idea on the remote chance that one day her fortune would change, and she would be allowed to walk through colourful scenes without fear, pain and the cold. Yet in these moments, her mind was as blank as it ever was, and although her eyes twitched open slightly, she did not see through them, the information that was taken in through her eyes was not transmitted to her brain in any conscious manner. Her ears though, her ears always stayed awake: she found herself to be increasingly sensitive towards aural data, in the same way that mice never truly sleep when there is an ever awake cat on the prowl, and at night she stayed in a dormant state of readiness of flight or fight. The fact that she could do neither did not deter her. On this occasion, her ears did indeed pick up murmurings below – perhaps it was in the room below, perhaps further down, or in a corridor, she could not be sure – and it was the presence of this that dragged her from her blank stillness.

Voices. Unrecognisable voices. Male voices. One deep, and grave; the other, hesitant, delicate.

"And no progress as yet?" This was the larger of the two voices.
"No." A long pause. "What do you suggest?"
"Not even with the…"
"No, sir."
"Have you got the reports there?" An assortment of noises. Creaks. Eventually, "I see."
"He's been very compliant."
"Good."
"But as you can see…"
"Yes, yes, I can. It seems we need something more…let us say…drastic. Desperate measures and all that. What do you think?"
"It appears to be what's needed. What did you have in mind?"
"Well can we use this…what's his name?"
"The brother, sir?"
"Yes, yes. Oh, wait a minute. Observation? Is it continuing?"

"Yes, sir, there's a man stationed outside at all times, he writes a very accurate account of the different aspects of behaviour. We had to allow him access to the…you know…*evidence*."

"Oh yes?"

"But it seems to have paid off, well we think so anyway."

"That's good then."

"Actually, sir…there was something we had in mind, that might interest you."

"What's that?"

"Differences have been observed between night and day, sir. We were thinking of implementing the same sort of strategy as was used for the Stoker case, if you remember, of 1992."

"Now let's see…yes, yes, I think I know what you're referring to. Yes. Quite remarkable, I think, if I remember rightly. Quite a success. Don't know why more didn't get excited about it, but it caused quite a stir here didn't it?"

"I wasn't here at the time, sir."

"No, a bit before your time wasn't it Gary. Yes well, *I* remember it anyway. You say there's no one else we can use?"

"No, no one else has managed to provoke a reaction as of yet. There's no one else we can try, at any rate. Was there…?"

"No, not at all. Forget it. The Stoker case, eh. Yes. Well. That ought to do the trick. When can he be expected?"

"He phoned earlier, sir, and said he would be coming up around half one."

"Oh good, so he'll be here soon then?"

"It seems so, sir."

"Good. If we can get this one cracked, you'll see the kind of media circus that something like this can create, if all goes according to plan. You might even make a name for yourself, Gary. That'd be something to write home about, eh? Well I can't stay long, as you know, dashed important business that I've got in the morning, must be off, you know. One can quite forget time in this place. You'll let me know how it goes tonight?"

"Of course, sir. I'll send you the paperwork as soon as it is done."

"Good lad. I'll be seeing you then."

"Thank you sir, and a pleasant trip home."

Movement could be heard below. The conversation had not penetrated comprehension in the woman's mind: the interplay of voices below had troubled her, in their interweaving music of textures and volumes. As she lay awake, shivering, her soft skin hitting the cold, callous stones that she laid upon, she could only envisage the figure that she had seen on the boat. She had now witnessed the same repeating scene five times over of the boat's approach to the building, and five times of its departure, and it had not become any less chilling or threatening – indeed, the spectacle had deepened, and she was now able, in its approaches, to pick out a slight drooping of the head, and the glint of light that picked out one of the eyes that stared out from the blackness of the face, and that told her he was watching her, he knew who she was and he was coming for her, and that all of his travelling to and fro was an elaborate prelude to her inevitable and glorious death. She feared it and the stranger immensely, but could not bring herself to do anything else but accept her fate. On many occasions, the peculiarity of the feeling that the stranger created in her made her stand, stock still in the middle of the room, and stare at the blue square, with dread and horror at the vibrancy of the colour and the insolence of its existence as something that was designed to delight, and bring peace to the hearts of human beings. She looked, always, for the boat to pass through it again, so that she could know for certain that her last hour was upon her, and in such revelation, she completed the final acts of her life and bid the world and herself farewell. But that last hour always passed, and the boat always departed. And as she stood, and watched it go, sensing how the robed traveller looked over his shoulder and let his ravenous teeth grate in frustration against each other underneath the darkness, she did not know how to feel, and simply sunk to the floor and watched her reflection in the mirror, to see what would happen.

This time she did not have to stand, and witnessed the boat leave from her position on the floor. Her gaze lowered to the mirror. She was barely visible. She let the darkness swirl around her and closed her eyes again.

The door opened. Its obstinate moan as it slid open woke her instantly, and she could not prevent her eyes opening, despite her efforts to always keep them closed on the moment of waking. The visitor closed it and it let out another pained wail. She watched the shoes shuffle over and settle themselves on the chair. Her gaze rose, and she took in the sight of the visitor, who clutched an old fashioned candle holder, and a candle, whose small flame flickered, being assaulted from every angle by the freezing air and the stuffy atmosphere.

Something felt different this time. The air was not the same air as it had been a few moments ago. It was sublime. It was different.

She let her eyes fall back to the shoes. She could be friends with the shoes. They did not look like unfriendly shoes.

"You should leave," she said.

There was a long time in which nothing was said. She did not want to take in the visitor's expression, and the shoes did not look any different, so she understood that he was not expecting her to say such a thing as she had just done. She let herself lie in a fatigued state of watchfulness, like a lazy cat.

"Why don't you lie on the bed?" he said. Silence. "Please, darling."

"Why don't you fuck off?"
"I'm trying to help you, darling."
"No, you're not."
"Please, darling, let me help you, sleep on the bed, it's not good for you on the floor. At least, let me give you a blanket or-"
"No."

The sound seemed to reverberate through the room. The shoes moved together.

"Or-"
"No."

Outside the wind seemed to be charging at the building, and the woman tried to imagine leaves being stolen from the grass and allowed to fly through the air, and become bruised and torn by the battering forces of nature. But there was something about the idea that did not allow the images to come to her mind, and she remained only with the sounds of the whooshing and whirling of the gusts to hint at a world outside her own.

"I've been thinking about you."
"I've not been thinking about you."
"Darling…"
"I haven't."
"What went wrong, my dear? Where did all of this come from?"
"Don't try it."
"What's wrong?"
"Don't try to bury into my soul. You can't, I won't let you."
"Why would you ever think I would do such a thing, my dear?"
"You're working for them now. I know it. You can't fool me."
"Them?"

"You're a fraud."

She could see the candle was having trouble asserting itself here. The coldness wrapped itself around the small light and it ducked and faltered as it tried to escape the blows of the home side.

Sigh.

"Tell me about her."

Silence. For a very, very long time. The woman stared at the shoes, trying to channel her rage into them, to set them on fire. They sat there, twitching.

"No."
"Why not?"
"No."
"What are you afraid of?"
"No. No. No. Fuck off."
"Is she…"
"Don't."
"Does she…"
"Don't say another word."
"And when she…"
"Shut up, now, or I *will* kill you, I don't care, I will fucking kill you if you don't shut up now, get the hell out of here, now, or I will fucking kill you. Now. Get out."

He paused. She thought she heard him lick his lips. "Can I meet her?"

"You goddamn son of a bitch."
"Could I…call her by her name?"
"What do you want from me, hmm? What do you want? Do you want me to die? You want to kill me, don't you, you want to rape me, you want to destroy me, you fucking maggot. You want to worm your way through me, don't you, well you can't, it doesn't matter what you say, I won't let you."

Her gaze was still the same. As she spoke her words were firm and angry, but she did not direct them towards him, but rather stared into space, disconnecting herself from the reality of what was going on and trying to escape into an existence far more pleasurable. And, she thought, he will not let me leave. For all of his confidence, it seemed he was now crying, and she would not have noticed, other than the dark, gritty tears that began to fall into her line of sight, and trickle down his trembling shoes. It was put on, she thought, he doesn't want this any more than I do. But she stared still, at those dripping shoes, and did not alter.

His sobbing went on for minutes. The ends of his trousers shook above his shoes, and soon his legs and feet were quite violently fluttering, an ever present pulsation of misery creating tremors through his entire body. After some time, his sobs did subside, although it seemed they would never do so.

"Please, darling, can't you tell me…"
"For god's sake shut up."
"Remember all the times, darling, everything we've been through together, you can tell me, you used to tell me everything, dear, don't you remember?"
"No."
"You do. Think about your memories. I'm in them."
"You think I want to remember? How you tried to set me up, you've had no clue, you always had no clue, you never knew me, you –"
"Set you up?"
"Yes."
"When?"
Pause. Annoyance. "You remember. Don't play games with me."
"I'm being honest. I don't remember."
"It wasn't that long ago."
"That never happened."
"Sure. Whatever."
"Are you okay?"
"Never been better."
"They told me you've been having problems. Why didn't you speak to me before, darling?"
"I wanted you to fuck off."
"Oh, dear…please don't."
"Why, am I breaking you? Is it too hard to take? Your little sister, finally she's found happiness, and you can't deal with it, suddenly all this shit has to happen, let's grind it out of her, and you have to come and sit there so pathetic, dribbling and snivelling. Just leave me alone."
"Happiness?"
"Yes."
"You're happy?"
"Yes. Too much for you?"

"No. I just thought…"

"What?"

"Can I…can I meet her?"

"No. I've told you. You shouldn't even be here now."

"Will you…will you ask her something for me?"

"No."

"Please, darling, if you loved me, you would do this one thing for me."

"I don't love you, and I'm not going to do anything for you."

"Oh…my dear…please…just…it's just, my dear…they told me today, that if you can get your…um…this girl of yours…if you can get her to come in, any day, and tell the people here that she can take care of you, they'll let you leave. I was going to ask…if you would ask her to do that for you, because I've got this…what with…auntie Alice passing away…there's a cottage…you see…that you can live in with her, and I thought that, well…you'd like that. Better than staying here, I thought. You don't ever have to…see…me…again…if you…don't want to. Just you and her together, none of this. Well I've…got to go. But I'll be…I'll see you again, my darling. Okay?"

The shoes pointed away. One left, then the other. Light steps, as he passed to the door. A sigh. Stifled sob. Moments passed in stillness.

"I…I love you, dear."

Then he was gone.

16

Somehow the night would not end. The woman, as she led, her body shaking against the cold floor and her teeth biting into her lip as they chattered, felt that truly, the world had become stalled between two days and that this was the night, the night laid out before her now, was the one from which no one would wake. Her eyes had stared into the same blackness now for hours, and she had listened to her lungs take in and expel breath for what seemed an eternity. It seemed that no one else on this earth dared breathe as she did, and that in her disturbance of the air instigated by her very existence, she struck a discord into the atmosphere of time, and space, and everything. She alone breathed, for every soul that had ever done so; and she alone saw into the unending, cloaking darkness, which every soul that had ever lived upon the earth had seen. Yet she drew breath unlike them, she saw what those before her could never see: and as she remained, like a black cat with illuminated eyes in the overpowering and almighty darkness, she let the blackness around her work its sublime magic over her, and weave its way into her mind and her soul.

She embraced her role as the rebel. Everything around her was so still, so quiet, and was set in such a state, timelessly, unchallenged. She alone could change that, she alone could keep the darkness here, a friend to draw to her breast and keep there always; she alone could make permanent this lingering night so that no one would ever wake again, and no day would ever dawn to trouble another lost soul like hers. Yes, this was it, this was her moment: her movement, freeing her cold limbs from their shivering binds, seemed so natural to her – a feline jump from inactivity to doing, to *being*, that signalled her birth into a new state, a new existence. To the bed, at once, the bed – thoughts ran thick and fast through her mind, each penetrating the silence of the darkness – and throwing her arms out she scratched at the covers, pulling each off of that resting place where she had never rested, until she was madly clawing at the brilliant whiteness of the sheet. Off, off, off it came, shining as distinct and as white as the woman's bared teeth that chattered helplessly no longer, but instead opened wide, gleaming, dripping with hunger and excitement. Then she held it, having been torn free of the mattress, its master, in her trembling, bony fingers – and it was all hers, a prize that left her dazed and triumphant. What power, she thought, as her hands slid down its unworn fibres, caressing its smooth freshness – an unscented, unmarked, innocent being. That sheet had laid there beneath those covers, seeing neither day nor night, gaining no impression of the world or of the body that it expected to accommodate – and now it lay in her hands, and was entirely at her command. She played with it, toyed with its limits, hugged it around her body and bit it to see if it would rip; and then, after she knew it, like it was an old friend, she laid it out in front of her so that it took up the most part of the floor. She allowed herself one fleeting, considering look at that white child's play mat, the squashed cloud, the soft white void: then began rolling it, from the longest side towards the other. And there, she sat, with this rolled up sheet, looking from one end down the white line to the other, and paused for a minute, before she began to tie a knot in it.

*

"It's been so long, Clarity."
"I know, I'm sorry, my love, it's been getting harder-"

"It's okay."

"I'm very sorry, my love."

"Clarity?"

"Yes, my love?"

"Talk to me."

"What about, my love?"

"Anything. Tell me…tell me anything. I want to hear your lovely voice play its music through my ears."

"I…I don't know what you want, my love."

"Talk to me, Clarity. Anything."

"I…I love you."

"I love you too, Clarity."

"I…I…I'll always love you."

"I'll always love you too, Clarity. Isn't there…isn't there anything you can talk about?"

"I don't think so, my love."

"How about…how about your family, you've never even told me anything about them. Where you come from. What you did today. Anything, Clarity."

"I…well…there's. There's nothing, my love. I can't…I can't."

"Well…if you can't, then just make it up. Talk to me about…anything made up. I don't mind. Lie to me. I just want to hear you."

"I…I can't."

"Oh…okay. Will you…? Can you. Just…hold me, Clarity."

"Yes, my love."

"Don't you want to?"

"Of course, my love."

"I love you…your…your warmth. You're always warm, Clarity. You make me feel warm too. I'm always warm when I'm with you. Cold when…you make me feel so…warm. Clarity."

"I love you."

"I love you too, Clarity…why…why do you? Maybe I don't want to know. When did you start? Maybe I don't want to know that either. Oh my love, my dearest girl, my deepest darkness, you can't understand what's happening to me."

"You want to talk about it, my love?"

"Yes…but also no…I…do you…do you ever get sad, Clarity, like you used to when I first met you?"

"Yes, my love."

"All the time?"

"Yes, my love."

"How does it feel?"

"Sad, my love. Very, very sad."

"Yes…that's how I feel…but why do I feel like this…when you're here beside me? Is it just the thought of leaving you again that fills me with all of this misery?"

"You were sad before me, my love."

"Yes…you're right."

"Sad after me."

"Oh no, Clarity, nothing ever after you…we live and die together. Don't we?"

"Yes, my love."

"Say something else, Clarity. Please."

"I…I love you, my love."

"Why isn't that enough anymore?"

"Sorry?"

"Why isn't enough to hear you say that anymore, I wonder. I don't love you any less yet…I can feel you slipping away from me Clarity. And I hate it. They're dragging you away from me I know it, first this - what else next…why can't you comfort me, why can't you hold me…"

"I am holding you, my love."

"Hold me tighter, then, kiss me, kiss my cold skin, warm it like you used to…why do I wonder whether this is our last night together, our last dance of pleasure before the day gives way to death…why, why Clarity, has everything changed so suddenly?"

"You seem different, my love."

"Do I? I suppose I am, I suppose I am. I…god I feel so awful. It's not right. You're here. I should be happy. But I'm not."

"Is there anything I can do, my love?"

"I don't think there…well. Actually…Clarity? If I asked you to do one thing for me, would you?"

"Anything you ask, my love."

"Could you…could you come in, tomorrow night?"

"To see you, my love?"

"No, no, not to see me – to go to see them downstairs, to tell them…to tell them you've come to take me home."

"What?"

"Don't you…don't you understand Clarity? They'll let me go. They'll let me go, only they want you to come here, so they can let me go with someone, with the girl I love. They need that Clarity. I need that, Clarity. I need you to come and rescue me. Nothing else means more than this to me, will you do this for me, and set me free from this place, so we can go and live together, live like freed birds together out in the countryside, out in the wilderness...free to make love out in the open...free to do whatever we want, be what we want, go where we want, wouldn't you do that for me, Clarity, will you come tomorrow and tell them not to hold me here any longer?"

"I...I'd love to, my love..."

"Would you? Will you do this for me Clarity? Oh, I knew I could count on you, my love, my soul, my breath, I knew they were wrong when they said that of you, all those times that they –"

"...but I can't."

"What?"

"I can't."

"Why not? Oh Clarity, don't forsake me now, don't you love me? Don't you feel *anything* for me? Can't you see I'm *dying* here? Can't you save me?"

"No, my love. I'm sorry."

"Why...why, my sweet bird...?"

"Because...my love, I'm not –"

"Don't say it."

"My love?"

"Don't."

"I'm sorry."

"I know, Clarity. Believe me. I know more than anyone. I suppose if I had to choose, I would rather be here with you than out there without you. Will you ever...will you ever come again, Clarity? Or is too strong...?"

"It is getting harder, my love –"

"I know, but is it too much?"

"I fear this will be the last time, my love."

"..."

"I'm sorry, my love."

"...I..."

"Can I do anything for you, my love?"

"Are you holding me already, Clarity?"

"Yes, my love."

"Are you holding me tightly, Clarity?"

"Yes, my love."

"Then...then kiss me, Clarity, kiss me all over, and love me like you used to, do the things you used to...maybe these last few moments of shameful and lonely ecstasy can bring some comfort to my cold, groaning heart...scratch it out, Clarity, scratch out my heart, I won't need it anymore, not where I'm going..."

"I..I love you, my love."

"God. I love you too, Clarity, and if I can love you no longer, then
I shall love the idea of you, and let my thoughts live with the dream that
has been you finding me, and loving me, and seeing me, all these blissful
days. Days in which I never knew what happiness was, despite the fact I
felt it; and though I could not leave my misery at bay, I now know I was
happy, very happy indeed, a happiness that to me is now just a word, that
provokes no feeling, and gives me no comfort whatsoever…keep going
Clarity, keep going, keep spreading your lovely darkness over me, let me
feel your sweet heat before the chill of sunlight finds me here, keep
going, oh I love you Clarity, I love you, I love you, I love you, I love you,
sweet girl, precious girl, oh, my fleeting dream, my Clarity. My Clarity.
My Clarity."

17

A worn, trembling hand pulled back the makeshift curtain from the
battered and stained window, to allow the coming sunshine to
cascade through in all its playful exuberance. Like a morning
fanfare it leapt through the room, filling every lingering darkness that
dared skulk about the floor, outstretching its warm gaze over those
forgotten things that lay huddled together as if searching for such a
comfort. The man closed his eyes and for some moments, he let himself
enjoy the sun's rays on his face that had for so long only been acquainted
with the cold sting of despair and misery. The sun was rising yet.

He let his old, frayed, abused clothes slip from his skin. It was not
such an effort – indeed, it had been, to draw them close over his
protruding bones, to hide his torment and shame; but now, now that he
stood in the full light of the sunshine, his body growing by the day to
cover properly that tortured, bony frame that he had lived in for so long,
all he had to do was to stop clinging the dirty rags to himself, to
straighten his spine, uncurl his tense fingers, to relax his arms and legs
and hold his head up to meet the day, and the rags soon began to fall, to
slide slowly over his skin, each piece sighing its goodbye to their prisoner
as they relinquished their only link to life. They fell in pieces, they fell in
silence, they fell like a dead and weak wrapper of used skin that was no
longer needed, and they met their graves upon that familiar cold floor,
and would be picked up no more, cling to the last murmurs of heat no
more, to be asked for their miniscule comfort no more. The fabric pulled

away from open wounds that were now healing over, soldering with the nourishment of new life, the blood to be wiped clean and the time for scars to form and fade now upon him. And there he stood, like a child again in the eyes of the power of nature that shined through that window, that welcomed him again into the world as its own, that lavished the sun's rays upon him so that he might shine like it too, and become the child of the sun here on earth. Born into the heat of that burning fire so far away, his body breathed with sensation as it stood, whole and proud again, embracing the warmth of the rays that blessed him and welcomed him into his new existence. His skin tingled, shocked as it was to experience the true power of warmth, having laid so long amongst the dirt and the cold; and it smoothed every part of his body, opening him out and propping him up from the shrivelled insect of a man that he had become. He stood, alone, while the sun rose, and felt the relief of a sentenced man who had been given another day to live, to breathe, to feel again, and he saw the beauty in everything.

He pushed open the door to the room – that had been for so long *his* room, now to relinquish that state of occupancy once and for all – and ventured to open the box that sat just outside. From it, he pulled his new attire that he held up at once to admire, and then proceeded to dress his liberated body with; loose, dark blue trousers, a plain white shirt, a purple waistcoat and a black hat, which seemed to sit so perfectly on his head. He looked up and down his clothed body and marvelled at the extreme difference between what he had come to know and what now met his eye when he looked down at himself: his legs seemed strangely inclined to jig about in his new, soft trousers; his arms poised at once to reach out, or to gesticulate, as if we were to make a momentous speech; and his head tended to look high up into the air, as if he were an admiral beginning to set sail on a new and exciting adventure, overlooking the calm seas that stood before him. Satisfied and ready, he pulled the door to a close, not pausing for a second to look back into the room for a last impression: he had enough memories to last him for the rest of his days, had he ever a need to think of his age-long confinements again. Down the stone steps he went, a spring in his step, despite the fact that fatigue and malnutrition had only relinquished their traumatic grasp over his body and soul within the last few days; his joviality could not be caged within his heart, and he did not want it to be, and so he let it flow through him, through his limbs and through his eyes, enjoying at every turn this rush of new feeling that had met him. He felt so loose, so capable of anything within these new clothes, and under them, he wore a similar set in his mind, that let joyous and free falling thoughts run wild and giddy, completely intoxicated as he was with the departure from his tortuous ordeal. It was over, it was over, and he had a chance to live again: and to live, to think about the possibility of *living* again, had been such an impossible and improbable circumstance for so long now that the overturning of this scenario had near knocked all the breath from his lungs and filled him with a permanent sense of rapture and purpose. He was to live again, he was to enjoy the experience of existing again, he was to laugh, to jump, and dance, and smile, and feel waves of happiness and love course through his body that had almost forgot such feelings existed, all of this and more was to happen to him, *him,* and it was a true a promise as the rise and fall of the sun. He was quite overwhelmed; and had spent much of his time, within the last few days, modulating between physical unrest and audible expressions of delight and relief, and between sitting quite still, considering the reality of such a promise, and crumbling into joyous tears forthwith. Now, however, he was quite in the former mood, and bounced down the steps of the tower with carefree movements and an ecstatic smile upon his face.

He pushed the door at the bottom of the tower open, to reveal himself truly to the world of summer, and light, and life. The freshness of the air was quite staggering as it rushed into his lungs, and he looked on his surroundings with new eyes, for he could not remember ever being here before, looking as he did now, at the environment laid in front of him: a shifting field of fire waved, and leaped, and pirouetted in its ever burning celebration of life; beyond, the other towers rose from the fiery bed, cold and sullen, refusing to be lit by the dangerous energy of the luminous dance below; and even beyond that, the great, circular wall stood, all encompassing, a grand, stone circumference. A few moments were needed to gulp down the new scenery, while drinking in the cool, sweet air. Waking from his shock, his eyes focussed on his surroundings close by, and was greeted by the sight of a boat, waiting patiently at the small dock. Within it, looking away from him, seemed to sit a boy, who held the oars, and whistled lightly, and sitting opposite, looking towards him – if the being could look – was that familiar heap of black robes, who had been for some time a regular yet silent visitor. The man wasted no time in departing from the cold stone tower, and relished the moment when his feet left the platform: the boat then rocked as it left, travelling slowly then swiftly through the sea of jumping flames.

The journey was quite extraordinary, yet entirely impossible to recall to mind at later instances. His mind buzzed, a kind of electricity that resulted from his excitement, that permitted no conscious thoughts about anything or anyone – he simply sat, inane grin upon his face, letting the moving scenery wash over his eyes in a state of incapacitated joy and absolute mania. If anyone had uttered a word, he did not remember – it mattered not, for only one thing was held within his mind, and that was of his freedom, and nothing else could touch that, could permeate its power and importance. It seemed he had only just set his feet on the vessel when materialising before him was the great dock of the great wall. There was the line of boats, into which this vessel would slide, and lie calm and undisturbed, while the passengers would depart and go separate ways to carry on their lives, and there was the platform, on which, he noted with surprise and intrigue, there were a great many people gathered, all apparently looking at his boat, and him, with some pointing and jumping up and down. He could not fathom what sort of excitement his release and entrance into normal society would cause and why, but simply let the fact of their existence add to the passionate joy he felt within him. Eventually, the boat did slide in, and the man leaped, unable to wait a second longer, onto the platform, onto stable land once again, to the sound of a cheer from the crowd: he was met with smiles, and handshakes, and slaps on the back, and words of congratulation and even presents and cards expressing warmth and happiness. His eyes scanned the overwhelming mob to catch a face that he recognised, but there were none. He stayed for some time amongst those well meaning folk, thanking them each in turn, and eventually emerged from the crowd to walk meaningfully, and with elation and pride, towards the main doors that welcomed him into the great wall again as an acceptable citizen. Stood to the side of the doors, a little girl stood, in a bright blue dress, her hands behind her back, looking intently at the man. The man tipped his hat, feeling as he did that day that he could do no wrong, and indebted to every man, woman and child of society, and beamed, saying "Good day, my child!" To his surprise, she held his gaze, so powerfully that he came to stop and listen with increasing interest to the words that seemed to be tumbling from her mind towards him:

"Hello, strange man, I hope you are happy now," she said.
"I am my dear, and I hope that you are too, or can be soon, for it is a wonderful feeling."
"Can I ask you a question, strange man?"
"Yes, my child, what do you seek?"
"Your name, if you please." She held his eyes with such intensity and power. She did not shift nor blink, and her eyes seemed to grow almost bigger and he stood, enthralled by this small creature. He lifted his hat from his head again, and bowed, and said to that little girl,

"I am afraid I do not have a name, my child, for I am only a character."

With that, the man walked on, through those double doors, into the great wall, to start his life anew.

***

Other fiction titles from Arena Books –

The Girl From East Berlin
a docu-drama of the East-West divide

by James Furnell

Few novels appear on such a grand scale as this. What begins as an inauspicious chance meeting in an East Berlin art shop leads to an adventure exploring the many social and psychological aspects characterising the division of a great European capital. It is an encyclopaedia of the soul of a city; unlikely again to be described so comprehensively or in such depth.

ISBN 978-0-9543161-7-4   **£18.99 / US$ 32.99**

Two Days in July
a docu-drama of Claus von Stauffenberg's attempt to kill Hitler

by Stig Dalager

This gripping book, by one of Denmark's leading writers, presents the story of Claus von Stauffenberg's assassination and coup attempt against Hitler on 20th July 1944 with perhaps greater clarity and psychological insight than any straight factual account could succeed in conveying.

ISBN 978-1-906791-12-4   **£14.99 / US$ 23.99**

The Rocket's Trail
the untold horror story behind the first moon landing

by Nick Snow

A docu-drama by a leading reporter which blends a fictional hero with real historical figures as Wernher von Braun, Edgar J. Hoover, Eli Rosenbaum, and Arthur Rudolph, the director of the Saturn rocket programme and the only former Nazi to be expelled from America.

ISBN 978-1-906791-30-8   **£12.99 / US$ 20.99**

The Ubiquitous Man
travel beyond the brink

by Christopher Orland

A mesmerising high-tech thriller speculating on the field of commercial teleportation. The year is 2104 and the teleportation of people from one continent to another has become an expensive and controversial reality. Hotshot salesman Guy Rennix of UK firm *Tempus Biotronics* is offered a business trip from London to New York, travelling via the ultimate mode of transport with unexpected consequences.

ISBN 978-1-906791-15-5   **£14.99 / US$ 23.99**

Arena Books – Fiction titles

And The Waters Shall Cover The Earth
a tale of the drainage of the Fens

by Forbes Bramble

A magnificently poetic and atmospheric book, by an established novelist, describing the fens and fenland life in the 1690s. The authenticity of the tale is brought alive by the descriptions of the environment with its mists and distant horizons, its characters and their dialogue, in a way which few historical novels are able to match.

ISBN 978-1-906791-14-8   **£15.99 / US$ 27.18**

The Bear Pit
A Medieval murder mystery

by Andrew Barlow

A Royal murder mystery set in the early 15th century. This realistic novel demolishes the myths of the 'Age of Chivalry' in portraying England's princes as born in a 'Bear Pit' in the ruthless struggle for power.

ISBN 978-1-906791-29-2   **£14.99 / US$ 23.99**

Printed in the United Kingdom by
Lightning Source UK Ltd., Milton Keynes
138847UK00001B/2/P